SHANGHAI WIND

A GATEWAY TO LOVE NOVELLA

CHLOE T. BARLOW

DEDICATION

To my beloved husband,
You continue to support me and encourage me more each day. I love you, and I am so grateful that we have the chance to spend our lives together. Thank you for being mine.

To China, and the many wonderful friends I made there.
Ever since the day I first stepped foot in a winding Beijing alley, and nervously began walking behind my loving host family, I've wanted to write a story set in China. It is such a huge part of how I became who I am today. No matter how many years I studied this unique country's language and culture, or how many times I lived there, it has never ceased being a source of great inspiration to me.

To the entire *Pink Shades of Words* team.
Breast cancer has touched all of us in some manner. In my own small way, I try to do anything I can to help the cause, and to give voice to those living with the impact of the disease. Thank you for the chance to be a part of this anthology and to help you with your great work.

To Pam Rosensteel & all the amazing folks in Chloe's Crew.
Thank you for finding me the perfect muse for Colin! There is nothing quite like the joy of sharing the exciting experience of writing novels with my wonderful street team, Chloe's Crew. All of the Crewbies had great ideas for Colin, but Pam managed to take the prize!

PROLOGUE

Colin stared down at his empty suitcase, unable to will his body to move. Piles of tee shirts, boxers, books, notepads, and whatever other crap he'd brought across the ocean with him, filled his temporary room. They seemed to dare him to begin the process of returning home. Looking to his left, he saw Feng Huang's back as she quietly folded a pair of his jeans, preparing to place them in another part of his luggage. Her head was bowed away from him, making her black, shiny hair fall forward. Though Colin couldn't see her face, he knew she had to be as sad as he was.

He wanted to rip those pants away from her and hide them. If they began to pack away all his things, that meant he was actually leaving her. Time was moving more quickly than he'd like, every second taking him closer to a life without Feng Huang, or "Feng" as everyone actually called her. Every one of the eighteen years of his life so far had been without her. That didn't change the fact that since he'd met Feng three months before, he'd been pretty much obsessed with her. His hands clenched into fists, desperate to hold her against him.

Unable — and unwilling — to fight the compelling need to touch her, he walked over and took Feng's hand, pivoting her body to face him. Her bottom lip was twitching ever so visibly with emotion as her dark eyes scanned up and down his face, searching for some kind of reassurance he knew he couldn't give to her. Feng was only seventeen, and still very gentle and naive about so many things. Colin wanted to tell her everything would be okay, but how could he promise her their hearts would survive this separation when he'd never felt this kind of pain before either?

Finally fed up with waiting for him to speak, she threw the jeans on his bed and quickly encircled her arms around his waist, resting her cheek on his chest. Colin wrapped one arm around her and stroked her smooth hair with his other hand.

Spending the summer before college in Shanghai with the family of one of his dad's business associates had sounded like a jail sentence at the time. But there'd been no choice once his dad found out he'd been "damaging" the good Prescott name with surfing, drinking, smoking pot, and just generally messing up his life with what his father considered the dregs of society at Venice Beach. It was bad enough that Colin insisted on playing competitive beach volleyball with anyone willing to take on the challenge, but to actually spend time with these kinds of people — that was apparently unacceptable for a prince of Newport Beach society such as himself.

Colin didn't flatter himself that he was a rebel or that his behavior was based on any kind of principled stand against class rules. He just liked to have fun in any way it presented itself to him, regardless of whether that fit into his father's plans for his life, or not. The reason for Colin's questionable conduct didn't concern his family anyway. The only thing that mattered was that he was doing such distasteful things at all.

So his father shipped him off to Shanghai for the summer to stay with the Ji family. They were deeply respected and well-connected throughout China — and wealthy enough to afford the costly fine associated with having two children under their nation's "one-child policy." If Colin could behave himself for a few months, then he'd get his trust fund and could run off to the University of Southern California and live life on his own terms.

Yet, everything he wanted changed the day he'd walked off the plane and met their daughter Feng. She was the second very costly child, who was the lovely gem her family doted on and treasured. Her older brother was staying at Beijing University for the summer, which meant she was stuck with watching after Colin and tutoring him in Chinese.

Colin had watched her every day, wanting her more by the minute. She was so innocent and beautiful — so different from anyone he'd ever known. As much as he was immediately convinced Feng was perfect, he knew she'd felt pretty sure for weeks he was nothing but an awful, lazy, and spoiled American. When she finally surrendered to him and let him kiss her on a small footbridge during a day trip to the Nanjing Botanical Gardens, his whole world exploded. All that mattered was kissing her over and over again, until their lips were swollen and red from so much contact.

The mere thought of the memory made him lean back from her, so he could tilt her face up to his.

"What are we going to do, Colin?" she asked him.

"We don't have to decide right now. We have this moment, and we have to make the most of it. It will never be here again."

She nodded slightly, tilting her cheek into the palm of his hand. Leaning down, Colin pressed his lips to hers, allowing the soft flesh to calm his tormented emotions. Her tongue teased at the entrance of his mouth, making him groan when it met with his own. Moving his hands to the thick fall of her hair, he drank her in with the desperate need of a man lost in the desert who'd finally found a tiny source of water. Feng had already made him such a better person, but who would he be without her?

Her hands eagerly pulled at the hem of his shirt, shocking him back from her. As he searched her eyes for a clue as to her intentions, his stomach twisted with the desire building inside of him. He'd never pushed her beyond kissing, knowing she was incredibly inexperienced, but the determination on her face filled him with a powerful hope that she might be ready for more.

"Feng…what are you doing?"

"You're right. This moment may be all we have together. I want to be with you…completely."

"Are you sure?" he croaked out.

"Yes. Please, Colin."

He nodded, moving his hands to her shirt, sliding it up her body and off her head. Her small, but perfect, breasts were covered by a white cotton bra. After throwing her shirt on the bed, he bent down to kiss the soft mounds emerging from the top of the virginal fabric. Running his tongue across the hot skin, down to the covered nipples, he wet the cotton until he could just barely see the outlines of her enticing nipples, taut and hard beneath. Tiny goosebumps quickly rose across the soft flesh of her chest. Colin could hear her breathing increase to rapid pants, mirroring the now frantic beat of his own heart.

Feng reached her hands behind her and removed her bra,

giving him a chance to take off his own shirt. She held his eyes for an instant, before wrapping her arms around him again. The sensation of her bare skin against his was making him crazy already. He didn't know how he'd survive touching the rest of her body.

Colin had slept with a lot of girls already, but none that he'd cared about, or wanted, so powerfully in this way. He felt a potent yearning to make her feel good and to give them both the perfect memory they would soon need once he did finally have to go. If he could make her realize with his body the magical effect she had on him, which he had never been able to put into any form of words, then maybe she'd never forget him.

He stepped away from her and took her hand in his, leading her to the bed. It was littered with clothing, which he quickly shoved to the floor. She perched delicately on the edge, looking up at him with her big, brown eyes that always made him feel like he couldn't remember how to speak — whether it be in English or the Mandarin Chinese he'd been struggling to learn.

Her hands reached to his belt, undoing it with slow, careful fingers. The movement was like licks of fire, scorching his skin through denim. His hands joined hers, undoing the button, as she slid down his zipper. Though he knew her parents were gone to enjoy a night at the *Shanghai Beijing Opera Theatre*, the sound seemed to echo through the quiet room like a scream. Colin pulled his jeans down, leaving on his boxers. He knew she'd proposed this, but he didn't want to scare her.

Kneeling before her, he kissed her mouth deeply as he pulled down her skirt. She lifted off the bed so he could remove her panties. Easing away from her mouth, he ran his lips down the length of her neck, licking and tasting her soft skin. He took his time, kissing her shoulder, then sucking at each breast, before sliding his tongue down the flat length of her stomach. Colin looked up at her, reveling in the beauty of her wide eyes and slightly parted lips, before moving his hand between her legs.

He pushed into her slowly with one finger. She was wet, but so incredibly small, making fear squeeze at him briefly. He was terrified he might hurt her, and destroy this beautiful experience for them. That worry became overtaken by intense need when he felt her spasm around his flesh, gasping in response to his touch. Colin desperately wanted to replace his finger with the warm kiss of his mouth. He was hard already, but the mere thought of tasting her sweetness was so tempting he felt himself stiffen further. Even so, he held back, overcome with concern about scaring her with so many new things all at once. Removing his finger from her, she squirmed slightly at the friction, but her accompanying moan encouraged him to keep going.

Colin stood and with a deep breath, walked the few steps to the toiletry case placed in his suitcase. He had a condom in the inside zipper compartment, though he never imagined when he'd packed it back in Southern California that he would use it to make love to the most precious person he'd ever known. When he turned back to Feng, she was lying along the bed, naked and ready for him. His heart skipped around in his chest at the sight of her.

"What are you waiting for? Come here," she said, giving him a small, nervous smile.

Colin didn't answer, but he did walk to her. When he removed his boxers and put the condom on, her almond-shaped eyes got even bigger as she took in the sight of him. Even if he hadn't been sure she was a virgin before, her response just then would've assured it. He climbed on the bed with her, running his hands up the length of her smooth legs, opening them so he could slide his body between them. His hands moved further up her body, stroking the swell of each of her breasts. He almost lost all self-control when she began touching him in return — running her fingernails along his back, his ass, and thighs.

His cock had a mind of its own, reaching for her warm center, as if possessed. With only a gentle touch of her entrance, his whole body tensed in anticipation. Colin knew he wasn't the greatest guy, but if someone this sweet could want to be with him, then perhaps he had a hope of being a better person someday — maybe even a hero. With each inch, he slowly pressed into her, and with every kiss she gave him in response, he felt more and more invincible. Until he came upon a barrier impeding his movement and she drew in a sharp, pained breath.

Colin eased slightly out of her body.

"No, don't stop," she choked out. Her English was impeccable, even in this turbulent moment.

"But I don't want to hurt you," he whispered against her ear.

"You could never hurt me, Colin. I want this. I'm going to miss you so much."

"Use the name you gave me. My Chinese name. I love the way you say it."

He could feel her relax slightly beneath him as they spoke.

"You know I gave you that name because I thought you were so bratty and kept fighting me all the time about studying, right? 'Ke' means to fight and resist."

"Oh, I thought you chose it because you knew you couldn't fight how much you liked me."

"I never could fight it, Ke Lin. You were right. I like you so much. I want to share this with you, even if it's a little painful."

Understanding, Colin nodded and entered her again, this time breaking through and moving fully inside her with one quick thrust. She screamed out, sending a shot of pain through his own chest. But he kissed her and moved gently inside her until her breathing slowed and she met his movements gently beneath him. His body relaxed above her, allowing him to enjoy the sensation of completeness and peace that came from filling every part of her body. She moaned into his mouth as he slid in and out of her tight body. He moved his face away from hers so he could look in her eyes as he stilled inside of her.

So much of him wanted to tell her he loved her. The words were tickling at his throat, fighting to escape, but the coward in him took over. He used his mouth instead to kiss her temple and focused all his energy on making her enjoy the little time they still had together.

He felt her tense beneath him, her moans becoming louder and more intense, until her eyes flashed open in surprise and pleasure. His hand went to her hair, winding his fingers into it as he secured his lips on hers. They breathed each other's air, in and out, in perfect rhythm. She gasped into his mouth, clenching around his length and sending him to a world of warm light and intense pleasure.

After the feeling subsided, Colin gently rolled to her side. He disposed of the condom quickly, eager to hold her in his arms. She laid her head on his chest, and he kissed her soft hair, inhaling deeply.

"Are you okay, Feng?"

"Yes, that was perfect, even if you're still mispronouncing my name," she teased, her nose rubbing on his neck as she giggled.

"What do you mean? I thought I was doing well with Chinese. I mean, I actually studied it — more than I have with anything else I've ever done."

"Your tones still need work. The way you say my name, it means 'wind.' My name is a different tone, and it means 'phoenix.'"

"These tones are such a pain in the ass."

"There's that bratty fighter I like so much," she answered with a giggle.

"Wait, is that why you always sing that goofy song from *Dirty Dancing* when your parents drag us to do karaoke? *'She's Like the Wind?'*"

"Yes. I thought you'd get the hint. I guess it's too late now."

"It's never too late for you to make me better. Though I should probably be mad at you because that has to be my favorite song now, Feng," he added, carefully trying to make the word sound correct.

"That's a little better. Good for you. And I will be sure to make it my favorite song, too. You know, the characters for wind and phoenix are really similar." Feng began drawing the shapes of Chinese characters on his chest and the intimate touch made his stomach clench with happiness. "This character is phoenix, and this one is wind. The difference is that one has an 'X' and the other doesn't."

"That's perfect. Because in America, X means kiss. And that is something we will always be good at."

Feng looked up and kissed him in a way that was even more sensual and mature than any kiss they'd shared before. Some of her innocence was now gone, but it was his to keep, and that made him feel like the most powerful guy in the world.

After he broke their kiss, Feng looked at him with deep sadness in her eyes.

"What's wrong?"

"I hate that you have to leave. What will happen with us?"

"I'll find a way to be with you again."

"How?"

"I don't know that…yet. What if you go to college in the States?"

"I can try, but that would be really hard to do. My parents would hate that. And college is a whole year away…"

"Don't worry about that. I'll be waiting for you…because we *will* end up together. I promise you that."

CHAPTER ONE

Approximately Six Years Later

A soft, perfectly-groomed hand landed on Colin's chest, jarring him from the memories coursing through his mind. He gently picked it up, laying it down on the bed beside its owner. Colette's measured breaths in response confirmed the woman had finally fallen asleep. She was the French wife of Swiss banker and prolific embezzler, Francois Babineaux, which was the only important part of her identity as far as Colin was concerned. He was not here to have a good time — this was all business.

He eased himself away from her slumbering body and sat on the edge of the bed, allowing the slippery-soft Egyptian cotton sheets to cool his hot skin. Leaning down to rest one arm on his knee, he ran his other hand through his auburn hair.

His recent time in the south of France had lightened it with fiery, rust-colored streaks, but that was the only record of his time here that would remain. He only had a short time to complete his assignment. Collette could awaken next to him at any second, and there was no telling when the infamous Monsieur Babineaux would return to their chateau.

After quietly pulling on his pants and shirt, Colin quickly located Babineaux's study and proceeded to copy the hard drive from his computer. Next up was to photograph documents from his files. That was the easy part, though after so many rounds of playing this game, it was all feeling far too dangerously simple.

At least this assignment had been remotely challenging, seeing as Colette had played coy with him for weeks. Even though her signature French mystique made his efforts to seduce her take slightly longer than usual, there had never been any real denying she wanted him. She finally gave in, as they all did.

No one on the team would ever accuse Colin of being any kind of tech genius. That was for other people to worry about after he made his delivery. He was merely the collector, as well as the main distraction. Any thief can break in and steal documents, but it takes a true artist to use his charms over women to secure an invite to the mark's personal space.

At least that was what he told himself. The point was no amount of state-of-the-art security system or armed guards could withstand the overwhelming power of a spoiled trophy wife's desire to feel pursued by a young piece of ass.

He still had to check for any other hidden secrets in the less obvious spots — loose floorboards, underwear drawers, and finally, the safe. He opened it easily, as he'd secretly watched Colette lock her jewelry in it before meeting him in the bedroom.

"Jackpot," he muttered around the small flashlight in his

mouth.

Ignoring stacks of money from countries of varying origin, Colin instead pulled out ledgers and stacks of private communications. They were in French, English, Chinese, and German, but Colin wasted no energy trying to translate anything. There was no time for that.

A small hint of lighter blue outside the window suddenly warned of the impending dawn. Colin began rushing through as many documents as he could, hoping he was managing to get enough images before he needed to be out the door.

With a soft click, he closed the safe door, careful to return the dial to the same last number as Colette had selected. Colin indulged in a sigh of relief, but the feeling was short-lived as a stream of headlights flashed through the room.

"Dammit," Colin grunted out. He took a brief moment to secure all his materials and quickly scanned the room. Convinced there was no sign of his presence remaining, he sprinted to the back staircase. Taking the steps down two at a time, he spun off the edge of the banister, landing lightly on the hardwood floor beneath him.

In the distance, he could hear the front door open and the heavy feet of Colette's hefty husband.

"Au revoir, Madame Babineaux," he whispered, before opening the back window and sliding to the ground. He made it to his car that was hidden fifty yards away. This time, they'd given him a black *Jaguar XK* convertible. It went perfectly with his current bored British heir persona, and he had to admit he liked it very much.

Dialing Lexis's number, he wondered if he could persuade her to let him keep it for a while, at least through whatever next assignment she had waiting for him.

The sun was rising aggressively over the Mediterranean Sea

when Lexis's smooth and husky voice came over the line. It had been a long time since their physical relationship ended, but she still had a pull over him with just the sound of her voice.

"Well, if it isn't the suave Benedict Pemberton."

"Save it, Lexis. I still can't believe you stuck me with that dumb-ass name for all these weeks. It's bad enough when I have to pretend to have an accent."

"Oh, don't be so cranky. I'm glad you finally wrapped up with Madame Babineaux, her little hard-to-get crap has put me sorely behind schedule. I was starting to worry you'd lost your touch."

"Never a chance of that," he answered with confidence. There had only been one time in Colin's life when sex had meant anything to him. Every other woman was an empty reminder of just how perfect it had once been. That made all this so much simpler. If it would always just be fucking, he might as well end up with something good coming out of it. In this case, that was delivering on the very valuable evidence of the elaborate scam the infamous Babineaux was running.

"Glad to hear it," Lexis mused over the line. "And I have good news. I know you will love the name we have for you to use this time. I had Claude sneak by and put your latest assignment in your glove compartment. I know I usually try to be more careful, but I was just too excited."

Colin rolled his eyes before locating the envelope she left for him. All it held was the latest CD from the world famous Shanghai-born pop sensation, Princess Phoenix. But Colin would forever know her as Feng. The shock overwhelmed him, almost running him off the road.

"Lexis," he finally managed to force out of his mouth. "I really don't think I should handle this assignment."

"And why the hell not, Colin?"

"I know her. She knows me…"

"Which is exactly why I chose you for it."

"I'll have to use my real name, Lex."

She laughed in response before adding, "I told you I knew you'd like the name for this one."

"It's too dangerous."

"I've accounted for all of that. We've done it before. Remember your assignment in Vancouver two years ago? We just have to be sparing with your real identity, is all. I have a great cover story for you and am already disseminating it in Shanghai."

"You've thought of everything," he replied dryly.

"I always do."

"But…"

"You care for her. I know. Fact of the matter is, she brought this on herself, Colin. She got involved with this Stephen Long guy. He may be new on the scene, but it's already clear he's involved in all kinds of shit. You only have one job — figure out what that is, and get as much information about it back to me as possible. Either you do it, or I choose someone else that won't have any qualms about hurting her. You know how it works…"

"Yes. If a woman is on our list, she has no reason to be protected."

"Right. For all we know, you could be helping her separate herself from this guy. You'll have a great night together, and she moves on with her life as the perfect little princess you thought she was," Lexis spit out, each word hitting him like a spray of little bullets. Colin swallowed, allowing the silence to overtake their conversation. The Mediterranean sun was warming his skin, but he felt nothing but cold disgust with the whole situation. "Colin, answer me. Are you onboard?"

"Yes," he said, softly in response.

"Now get your ass to Shanghai. You have a party to go to."

Colin ignored the shame eating at his throat as he inserted the CD, which displayed Feng's angelic face, into the *Jag's* stereo. The face that consumed his daydreams and tormented his nights, even though he'd only seen it in the media for the last six years. Despite the already intense heat of the morning, Colin felt a shiver run through him as the sound of Feng's beautiful voice wrapped tightly around him.

CHAPTER TWO

"Thank you all for joining me for this celebration. I know I am new to Shanghai, but you have all welcomed me so fully, I feel like I'm at home. Which is good, because I plan to buy a whole lot of the city while I am here."

The room full of Shanghai's most powerful people smiled politely at Stephen's crass joke. Though he was full-blooded Chinese, Feng could almost hear them clucking to themselves that his "Americanness" was palpable. He didn't even need to open his mouth for them to know he was, at his heart, a Westerner.

Hell, they probably thought the years of touring around the world had changed her, too, Feng thought to herself. Leaving China had a creeping effect, seeping into your bones and making you a slightly different person by each day. They still loved her, and her family. Their stares were gentle with her, and she knew it.

Not so much for Stephen. He was taller and broader than

the majority of the men in the room, but that was mostly due to his Northern Chinese lineage more than anything else. His Western identity was more subtle, coming through in the manner in which he carried himself, or the way his clothes fit. Even the most miniscule aspects of him screamed outsider. But this invader had money to burn and power plays to peddle, making his rudeness somewhat forgivable.

Stephen was the incredibly handsome son of Beijing intellectuals who immigrated to the United States when he was a baby. It didn't matter that he may look like his Chinese parents. As far as this room was concerned, he was not really "Chinese," and everyone knew it. It didn't seem to faze him, though. He loved his New York roots and appeared to be having a hell of a great time playing the part of a loud American. This was his party, and he was making it clear he had every intention of enjoying it.

That's where she came in, along with all of her connections. They would adore Stephen by the end of the night, and she would hate herself just a little bit more.

Stephen held his glass high and continued, "But the greatest treasure I found while in this beautiful city is your own gem by the sea, the beautiful Princess Phoenix!"

Feng fought a grimace at Stephen's transition from his stumbling and stilted Mandarin Chinese to the use of her stage name. It sounded ridiculous and clunky in English, but that translation was what had sold millions of records worldwide and she knew it wasn't going anywhere.

The room started to cheer for their "princess," and she could see how all distaste for Stephen's rougher edges were quickly vanishing. They didn't even seem to notice him cringe when he took a sip of the traditional rice wine.

"Hello, Princess," a deep, velvety voice said, quietly from

over her shoulder.

Feng turned to see Colin Prescott. Her heart clenched in her chest and her throat caught at the sight of him. She knew Colin would be there — his name was popping up everywhere lately, so it was completely natural he'd be invited. Even so, it didn't change the powerful sensation that overtook her body upon seeing him.

The time apart had only added to his sexiness. His haircut and clothes were more grown-up, and he carried himself like he was James Bond. Yet, all she saw was the shadow of the young man who had stolen her heart years before. Colin's face may be the same, but she worried her suspicion was correct — that everything good about him was now buried under inches of practiced charm and opportunism. It appeared that during their years apart, he'd let his weaker impulses take over his life again. It would serve her well to remember that, if she was to make it through the night.

"Don't call me that."

"I'm sorry, I didn't know if I was still allowed to call you Feng. I've never met a superstar before," he answered with a nervousness that resembled a time machine back to their last night together. With a soft smile, Colin added, "You look beautiful."

The cheering hadn't subsided, but Feng was grateful for it now, because it drowned out the brutal confusion going on inside her brain...and body. Taking a delicate sip of her rice wine, Feng used the time to will her cheeks to cool down and her heart rate to slow. Times had changed enough in China over the past decade that it wasn't scandalous for a woman to drink much in public, and she desperately needed the support it gave her in that moment.

She had known this would be hard; the only way to get

through it was to forge ahead. Finally placing her glass on a table, she met his eyes. She couldn't figure out how almost six years — and so many questionable acts — had passed, and yet his beautiful, forest green gaze had never changed.

"I can't talk right now, Colin. Stephen needs me."

"Oh, right. Stephen Long. Some catch you have there," he said, with a sneer. "Did you find him in the douche bag section of the *Beijing Silk Market*?"

"You don't know him."

"Do *you*?"

The cheers were so loud they almost battled with the sudden pounding of the pulse in her limbs at being near Colin again. She could feel Stephen's eyes on her and swallowed hard. She needed a break — to be someone else for a moment.

Perhaps pretending to be a "princess" would help.

"Excuse me, Colin. I need to go onstage and sing. I have to do this," she added, wincing inwardly at the ironic truth of those words.

"You can't keep them waiting, I understand. But I'll wait for you. Right here."

"Thank you," she muttered out, as she alighted the small stairs with leaden feet. The warm spotlight covered her body, setting her skin and floor-length couture gown awash in a false aura of privacy. The effect still brought her a sense of calm, just as it had done since she'd began singing as a tiny child. She could feel her elaborately curled hair sliding across her shoulders as she moved to take the microphone from Stephen. He kissed her lightly on the cheek and she forced a smile in return.

After a deep breath, she drew her red lips into a broad smile.

"Thank you all for coming and supporting my new love,

Stephen."

Feng was deliberately speaking Shanghainese, the Chinese dialect of her hometown, letting the delicate sounds and complicated tones play across her tongue. It was a calculated move, as she was confident Colin would only be able to understand traditional Mandarin Chinese. She knew it would drive a dagger right through his practiced, laid-back charm. Colin fucking hated not knowing what was going on around him.

The cheers filled the room again and she blew Stephen another kiss. He held a hand to his heart in return. She felt relief at the sounds of feminine sighs and flashing bulbs in response. They were accepting Stephen as another master of the economic universe more by the second.

Turning to the crowd, Feng continued, "You are all my family. No matter where I travel, or what I do, I will always be a Shanghai girl, with Shanghai wind in my hair." Her eyes went to Colin and she caught his gaze easily. "I was going to perform one of the singles from my new album. But looking at all of you and seeing your warm welcome, I have decided to share one of my favorite songs from my childhood. It's called: *'She's Like the Wind.'*"

Turning to the band, she gave them a brief nod and they began to play the piece, just as she had instructed them hours before. It calmed her to see that Colin was clearly unsettled with the song choice. If she was going to make it through the night, she needed to keep him that way.

The limelight swept across Feng's ivory shoulders, illuminating the delicate features of her face. Colin knew her choice of song was deliberate. He assumed her desired effect was to make him feel like his heart was squeezed in a vise, and she'd certainly achieved it.

With each word she sang, he was more completely transported back to that last perfect night they were together, but also brutally reminded of how he'd never followed through on any of his promises to her.

Colin had spent the previous few weeks focused on securing an invitation to this event. He'd also tried to ready himself for the potent impact of seeing Feng again, but he had still been painfully unprepared for the experience.

Feng had acted like a tonic to his wild spirit, but unfortunately the effect had only been temporary. That summer he was near her, he'd been the best version of himself. Yet, no sooner did he leave her presence, then he began making one indulgent and questionable decision after another, until he was so far gone that he knew he could never try to be with her again.

All those reasonable conclusions he'd made to close the door on his feelings for Feng went out the window as soon as he'd lain eyes on her…smelled her.

Because just being near her made him wish again for all those other times and for the hope of whom he could have been.

She finished singing and kissed Stephen briefly on the cheek, sending a shot of hot anger through Colin's body. Only Feng had ever made him feel that way, and he wasn't good at dealing with it.

After Feng left Stephen, Colin held his breath as she walked slowly toward him, filling him with that same tingling sensation in his limbs he'd felt every day during their summer together.

"You did wait for me. How refreshing, Colin," she said, meeting his eyes firmly.

"That was wonderful," he answered, ignoring the implication in her words.

"Thank you. I wasn't sure if I'd remember it. I haven't sung it at all for almost six years now."

Colin lost his breath for a second, processing this information.

"It's still my favorite song, Feng." Her jaw clenched visibly in response, and he committed to another tactic. "You sound amazing no matter what you sing. I bought all your albums."

"Did you even buy my albums in Chinese?"

"Especially those. It was my way of listening to your voice again."

"Colin…" She turned away from him and the confusing feeling inside of him got even stronger. All he could do was keep on talking and hope it would pass.

"I even got your kids album. Though I definitely felt awkward buying it on *iTunes*."

"True, you aren't exactly the target audience…for any of my music, really."

"You never had any trouble getting me to listen to anything you sang," he replied, before adding, "I must say, I'm pretty shocked to see you with a guy like Stephen."

"Well, I guess no one knows about my bad taste in guys as well as you do."

"Ouch."

"It's not an insult. It's the truth. You don't know anything about my life now, Colin."

"I want to know about it, though. We have a lot of catching up to do. I can't walk away from you yet."

Feng looked back at Stephen across the room.

He was surrounded by a dozen people, and seemed to be very busy laughing too loudly and apparently completely ignoring his beautiful girlfriend.

When her eyes met his again, that gentle hint of warmth that had been lacking all night shimmered slightly.

"Okay. Let's go and talk."

"Really?"

Her sudden compliance shocked him, but he didn't mind it.

"Yes, really. Meet me outside. I will tell Stephen I am tired and need to go home." She turned and left before Colin could do anything but follow her instructions.

CHAPTER THREE

Feng could barely unlock her door without giving in to seemingly suffocating and conflicting sensations of want, disappointment, and fury. She hated how those emotions still plagued her at the mere thought of Colin, even after all those lost years.

She and Stephen had secured a palatial, modern suite in the *Park Hyatt Shanghai* for their time in the city. Walking in with Colin close on her heels, she felt like it might as well have been a closet, because being in the space with her first and last love, was oppressively claustrophobic.

Feng poured a glass of French wine and walked across the room. She stood in front of the floor-to-ceiling windows overlooking the Huangpu River, cutting a path through the bustling metropolis and sparkling lights of her ancestral home. Colin's face was reflected in the glass before her, but she kept her back to him.

Clutching at the stem of her glass, Feng tried to refocus

her anxious thoughts on why she'd asked Colin to return with her. It helped to remember what a small part she was of the expansive world beneath the glass.

So many millennia of history had occurred in this city by the sea. Empires had risen and fallen, lives were made and destroyed, and loves had been gained and lost. Perhaps many true princesses had looked out over that same water, as the Shanghai wind blew through their hair, with their own worries for the future. Feng and Colin were just two small, lost souls. No matter how much this would hurt, their times, too, would pass.

She continued to watch his beautiful reflection in the glass, as he fixed himself a cocktail from the bar. He approached her; trapping her breath in her throat. Feng tried to tell herself he wasn't real, rather he was just a perfect mirage taken straight from so many of her heartsick dreams, because it hurt too much to know he was really there, yet he was not hers.

"No fiery glass of Mao Tai rice wine this time?" Colin asked, his slightly teasing voice breaking through the silence.

"When no one is looking, I do what I want, Colin. You should be pretty familiar with that kind of life."

He winced, before responding, "I get it. You hate me."

"How I feel about you isn't important. Point is, I don't have to be a perfect Shanghai songbird princess when I'm here."

"Oh. Um, when does Stephen come back?"

"Not for a long while, probably not until tomorrow morning, but what do you care?"

"You're so different now, Feng — so cold."

She wasn't cold at all. In fact, she'd been burning up since the first moment she caught sight of him. No matter how much she tried to remind herself of what her plan was, that teenage lovesick girl inside her wanted to throw herself into his arms. She yearned to tell him all was forgiven and ask if they could begin again. Yet, that girl was dead, and she had much more important things to do now.

"I've grown up, Colin. When a broken heart heals, the scar tissue has a tendency to deform the whole organ. Nothing is ever the same again. You'll find that a lot about me has changed since I was seventeen."

Colin put down his drink and moved his body in front of hers so she had to look at him.

"Don't say that, Feng. I hate how I broke my promises to you. I know I don't get to ask you for anything, but I can't help myself. I have to believe I didn't break who you were."

"Then maybe you shouldn't have ignored me when I went to America. I kept my end of the bargain. You never told me you'd changed your mind in any of your emails or phone calls. Maybe it took me three years, but I came to you!"

"I know you did. I went back to all my old ways so quickly as soon as I left you. Then I dropped out of college and lost the beach volleyball Olympic trials. I ran through my trust fund and started fucking up even more. But I always told myself I'd be able to fix things and be a good guy when you finally arrived."

"Oh, so it's my fault?"

"Hell no. I wanted to believe I wouldn't destroy myself too much before you came, but I failed. And then I made a choice I couldn't undo. By the time you came to America, I was in too deep."

"Too deep? Into what?"

"I can't say."

"And that's why you just ignored me? You know what, never mind. It doesn't matter. After that, I moved on and forgot about you."

"No, you didn't. You couldn't have, because I've never forgotten about you. Regardless of how much I fucked up, we will always be a part of each other. After I made the choices I did, I knew I couldn't be with you. I didn't want to let my life destroy you, too."

Feng couldn't control herself for another second more.

"I *have* to move on!" she yelled. "I have to be able to forget you and be different from who I was, because if I don't, then…then I can't do what I have to do. There is no choice for me here!"

The frustration coursing through her limbs was overpowering. She released a feral scream, as fury possessed every drop of blood in her veins. Her arm pulled back, seemingly of its own volition, and she threw her glass against the window beside Colin's body. The vast view disappeared for a moment, hidden behind spraying wine and slow-motion, flying shards of glass. Colin moved his back to the sharp glass, wrapping her in his arms to protect her from harm.

He stroked her hair slowly with one hand and the familiar sense of calm that came from being in his arms was almost as impossible to fight as the instinct of muscle memory.

"What do you mean, Feng?" he whispered.

"Nothing, forget about it," she mumbled, unknowingly falling back into speaking Shanghainese.

She looked away from him. None of it was supposed to go this way, but she couldn't help herself. He'd failed her in the most hurtful of ways, but all she could think of was that his lips still looked like home to her.

Feng was so overcome, that she had to deliberately force herself to begin speaking in English again.

"Why did you come tonight, Colin? Tell me the truth." Her

voice was cracking and her throat was thick from unshed tears.

Colin's penetrating, green eyes held hers, as though she were locked in a trance. He reached his hands to her face, placing them on her burning cheeks. His touch was devastating, and before she could stop them, silent tears fell from her eyes. They slid down her cheeks and baptized his comforting hands with her long-denied love.

"Feng, I came because I couldn't pass up the chance to see you…and I had to make sure you're okay. I was worried about you. I couldn't let you be with me because I am too much of a danger to you, but I refuse to let you be in a situation that could possibly lead to having any harm come to you."

"Stephen?"

"Yes. He's not who you think he is. You have to believe me."

"That's why you came? To make me breakup with Stephen?"

"In part. I also had to tell you that if I could, I would redo everything in my life after I left you. But, I wouldn't change anything about our last night together, except for…"

"Except for what?"

"I would've told you I loved you. I was too scared to say it that night. And I thought I'd do it when you came to America…"

Feng tried to look away, but he pulled her face back to his.

Colin began speaking again; this time in the perfect Mandarin Chinese she had once been charged with teaching him. The words shot into her heart like a flurry of arrows from an invading horde of Genghis Khan's men overpowering an ancient and unprepared Chinese capital.

"But I do love you, Feng." Colin hesitated, staring at her mouth as he stroked her cheeks with his thumbs. When he looked into her eyes, Feng lost all the fight left in her, because nothing would ever change the fact he was what she wanted the most in life.

As though he sensed the change in her, Colin kissed her lips lightly and she almost lost her balance. "I loved you then," he added, kissing her again. "I love you now," he whispered, before another brush of his lips on hers. "I will love you forever," he finally said.

Feng couldn't resist her need for him anymore. She wrapped her arms around his neck and kissed him with all the power left inside of her quivering body. Maybe the cruelty of fate and the weight of mistakes would mean they'd only get one more night together in this tiny blip of a lifetime. Even so, she had to take it, because a life without another perfect moment with Colin was no life at all.

Colin moaned into her mouth, before his tongue slid through her lips, forcing her to open to him. His hands fell from her face, quickly moving to grip her ass firmly. Feng gasped out when he deftly lifted her, and she wrapped her legs around his waist to keep from falling. The resounding echo of her expensive gown ripping at its already provocative slip accentuated the disoriented frenzy taking over each of her senses.

She couldn't see anything, all she knew was Colin was back in her arms and she was not going to let him go. He broke from her mouth and she tried to yank his face back to hers. Before their lips met again, he breathed out, "Where?"

"Anywhere. I don't care," she panted.

He smiled back, relaxing his hold so her body slithered like a snake down his front. It was so hard to look away from his red and swollen lips, so she blindly tugged at his tuxedo jacket, bow tie, shirt, and whatever else she could get her shaky hands on and removed it with a force she didn't know she had. Anything to be close again to his perfect mouth. Colin was just as eager, ripping at her already torn dress.

When they were both finally naked, Colin was frozen in place as he stared at every inch of her. Feng paused, too, desperate to look at his grown and fully-muscled body. Their hands tentatively explored each other's bodies. When he stroked and held her breasts, she groaned from the perfect feeling of tightening it provoked throughout her body. His soft hands moved down to her waist, tickling over her rib cage.

Feng's lips found his nipples, nibbling and licking at them. Her tongue tracked the curve of his pecs, trailing across his chest until she could bite his shoulder; loving the taste of him. Leaning back, she took in the amazing visual effect of her brief teeth marks on his ruddy and tanned flesh. His right hand moved to stroke her face, but Feng stopped her passionate tasting of his flesh when she saw a vibrant tattoo on the inside of his bicep.

"Colin…"

His eyes found hers, and they were wet with emotion. She cautiously raised her fingertips to the brightly-colored traditional Chinese design of a phoenix, rising from ashes and wrapped in smoke and wind. Beneath the image were the characters for both "wind" and "phoenix."

Looking back at him, Feng tried so hard to make a sound but every one of her words failed her.

"It's you, Feng. I've had it for years. I told you. I love you. It will always be you for me — even if we can't be together."

More gently than before, she leaned forward and kissed at the flesh of his arm. Then slowly, swiping her flattened tongue across his heated skin. Taking his hands in hers, she pulled him to the plush rug in the center of the room. It was probably worth a small fortune, but nothing was as valuable to her as their brief time together.

Colin kept her hands in his as he lay back and she quickly straddled him. The first time they were together, she'd been so timid, but she wasn't a scared teenage girl anymore. She was a grown woman with the added experience to prove it. Feng wanted everything from Colin and she was going to get it, because tonight would have to be enough to last her for the rest of her lonely lifetime without him.

"Whatever warnings you think you came here to give me Colin, we both know you're the real trouble I can't seem to stay away from," she remarked, as she sensually moved up his body, until she settled over his warm mouth. She could feel the expanse of his gleeful smile against her hot center. His strong hands gripped her hips, holding her firmly in place. He let out a deep breath as he brought his hands down; his thumbs separating her to allow his tongue complete access to her. The rough wetness of him against her sensitive flesh sent quick spasms through her body.

Rocking against his face, she arched her back and ran her hands through the heavy layers of her hair. His tongue was pumping into her wet opening as the contours of his mouth and nose teased against her clit. Her heavy groans resounded throughout the large suite when his mouth closed around her sensitive flesh. He sucked and released, each time harder than the last, until she felt drugged by the sensations his mouth was creating. His large hands returned to her hips, forcing her core to rub more powerfully against his lips and tongue.

"Mm-hmm," she panted as he labored on her slick center.

Looking down at him, she became fixated on the bright gems of his now sparkling emerald eyes. He was looking back at her with the same depth of emotion currently engulfing her.

Feng had replayed their one time together over and over in her head a million times. In her fantasies, she would often pretend she'd been much more bold. In those dreams, she'd made the most of the experience, rather than just being the shy virgin who didn't realize she might never experience anything like that again.

This was not her imagination, it was reality, and it was amazing. She grabbed his hands from her hips and placed them on her breasts, sucking on one of his fingers while she rode his face and fast tongue until her whole body shook on top of him, and an uncontrollable scream escaped her mouth. Her body bowed so much the ends of her hair tickled the tops of his thighs.

Suddenly, his hands were back to her waist and Colin was moving her back down his body. When her bottom reached his lap, he sat up quickly, throwing her on her back against the soft rug. Twisting his own body so he was kneeling between her parted thighs, Colin looked down at her, his nostrils flaring as he stared at her with a look of such ownership that Feng felt her heart and body open even more to him.

He reached over to his pants, pulled out a condom, and handed it to her. Feng opened it and slid it down his length. With his hands on her ass, he lifted her off the floor and entered her in one fast thrust, making her moan from the delicious feeling of him inside her again after so many years. She squeezed at him and moved with him, as he pounded rhythmically in, and out, of her body.

As intense as their need was, neither could be gentle with their movements, but their eyes never roamed — both remained fixed on the others' face, afraid they would disappear when this dream finally ended.

Colin finally slowed himself slightly, laying his body over

hers, so that when he stroked himself inside her, every inch of them was touching.

Meeting her eyes again, he smoothed back the hair from her face and whispered, "I'll love you...always." Then he kissed her in a way that spoke every word their mouths couldn't, as light streaked before her eyes and her whole body tensed beneath him. His muscles flexed hard against her hands. Colin broke the kiss, and his long groan vibrated against her ear, as he came with her.

After they both came back to earth, he rolled off her, pulling her alongside his body quickly before she could even think of moving away.

Feng rubbed her cheek against his firm chest and looked at their entwined bodies reflected in the glass of the window, the subtle hint of sparkling lights in the distance beyond them.

"I will always love you, too, Ke Lin," she whispered against his neck, before closing her eyes and letting the perfect feeling wrap around them completely.

CHAPTER FOUR

A distant, muffled sound and odd, lingering smell stirred Feng from her sleep. Caught between waking and continuing to doze, she rolled over and reached for the security of Colin's warm body. They'd found their way to the bed before they made love again, after which she'd allowed herself to fall asleep blissfully against his chest.

She'd never forget how much he'd hurt her, but there was no denying she wanted to forgive him. Although, she was trying to temper her thoughts, reminding herself they could only have that one night together, that pesky bastard, "hope," kept popping up and making her think there had to be some way they could keep from losing each other all over again.

All that stupid problem solving fled her brain when her searching hand touched nothing but empty sheets, cold from the absence of a body for some time.

Feng's eyes flew open with newfound alertness. Her teeth gritted against each other and her brow furrowed in determination. Feng pushed down the duvet and flung her legs off the bed. She silently pulled on a pair of black leggings and a tightly-fitting, dark tank top, yanking her hair into a ponytail with the barely contained cocktail of anger and shame swirling inside her.

Mouthing curses to herself in various languages, she became increasingly furious that the respite from her current life had been far too short-lived.

She knew better, but apparently, no matter what accomplishments she achieved in her life, when it came to Colin, she would forever be a stupid child.

Part of her wanted to go to sleep and pretend she'd never seen any of this. Maybe Colin would come back to bed…

No, she knew the warmth of lies — even those she told to herself — were mere false comfort. The only way to move forward was to face him. She'd handled unfortunate situations before. Pretending to have a stone heart had helped her in the past, unfortunately, she only had a broken one this time.

Each step of her bare feet took her closer to a truth she didn't want to know. But she knew she was braver than she appeared, which was good, because she needed that courage to survive the waiting sight of Colin hunched over a computer next to a pile of files in the suite's office. This reality was worse than any punch to the gut. His hands were moving so quickly, she could barely see what he was doing.

Her tears felt like pinpricks piercing her eyes and the air left her body in one large, silent gasp. She leaned against the wall in the darkness, trying to catch her breath. Her eyes squeezed tightly as the bone-crushing pain shooting from her stomach and into her limbs took over her senses. All was lost. There was nothing left to do but face him.

With her heart pounding so hard it shook her eardrums,

she stepped away from the wall and padded toward him. Its rhythm also pounded brutally against her sternum, as though a soundboard operator in one of her concerts had lost his mind, turning the bass up too high and destroying everything...for everyone.

When Colin turned off his tiny flashlight and began to straighten up everything around him — attempting to put the world right again — she made her move. She had to squeeze her hands into fists several times to make them work again, then found the panic button on her watch. Her thumb slid across the metal twice, and the painful failure of the moment made a silent burst of emotion twist through her throat.

Fighting through the pain, she pressed down firmly, knowing Stephen would be there to help her dispatch the threat at any second. That meant she needed to contain the situation until he got there. She could do that — had done it before, and would do it again.

Colin brought this on himself. Stephen was right, if they had gotten Colin's name as a target for this mission, then that meant he was already too far gone. She'd just been the dumbass who never stopped believing in the man she thought he could be.

Before she lost whatever nerve was left in her, Feng dropped to the floor and silently approached Colin from behind. He grabbed his bag and started to turn around. She went low, lunging at the backs of his knees with her right shoulder.

She'd trained in wushu martial arts since she was a child, but this was a move Stephen taught her. It may not be as elegant or beautiful as her Chinese techniques, but it was certainly effective. Colin's legs gave in immediately. He was strong and almost succeeded in regaining his balance, but she used her leverage to push him facedown to the floor.

"Feng, what the fuck are you doing?" he asked, trying to push her off his back. "I was just about to come back to bed…"

"Save it, Colin. I know what you were doing." All her sadness and disappointment from catching him in the act of using her to gain access to information on Stephen quickly morphed into pure, unadulterated rage. With a knee to his back, keeping him pinned to the floor, she reached over to a robe that had been left on the floor. After using the sash to rapidly tie his hands behind his back, she finally eased off of him a bit.

He struggled underneath her, twisting his head to look her in the eyes.

"You have to listen to me, Feng. It's not what it looks like."

"Wow. I really thought you'd be able to come up with a less clichéd lie. I must say, Colin, I'm quite unimpressed."

"If you'd just let me talk. I was trying to help you."

He managed to turn over and almost freed himself from her hold.

"*Help* me? Stop lying, for once in your damned life. I don't need you to tell me what you've been up to. I've seen the reports, even if I refused to believe them."

Feng couldn't listen to him anymore. The mere sight of him and his bag full of stolen information was already too much to bear. Reaching her forearm around the front of his neck, she found the pressure point to render him unconscious and silenced him.

She climbed off him, rolling him onto his back so he could breathe more easily before standing up on her slightly unsteady legs.

Stephen barreled into the room with his semi-automatic

pistol drawn; worry streaked across his face.

"Are you okay, Feng?" he asked urgently, rushing to her side.

"No," she answered honestly as she grabbed Colin's bag and handed it to Stephen. "I guess you were right about Colin, after all."

Stephen sighed sadly and returned his pistol to the hidden holster within his rumpled tuxedo jacket. He must've fallen asleep in it waiting for her to contact him.

"I didn't want to be," he responded gently.

He looked down at her and squeezed her shoulder, deep concern showing through his handsome features. Now that he didn't have to pretend to be an ass for their mission anymore, Feng could see again why so many women found him irresistible.

"I didn't want you to be, either. It's over. Yǒu yuán wú fèn," Feng mumbled to herself, as she slumped in a chair, staring at Colin's motionless figure. He'd come to soon enough, and she'd have to be tough and strong — she'd have to be someone else all over again.

"What does that mean?" Stephen asked, looking down at her kindly, clearly trying to get her head back in the game.

Feng forced a tiny smile.

"Stephen, some day you are *really* going to need to pay attention to the cultural side of your lessons."

"Come on, Feng, you know I hate that crap," he answered, desperately trying to lighten the surreal and dark mood.

"It's an ancient Chinese saying — an idiom, I guess. It means…well, it doesn't really translate, but it's when two people are destined to meet, yet fate will not let them be together."

Stephen made a face and finally responded, "See, this is

why I'm glad I grew up in America. We never let shit like destiny, or fate, or reality get in the way of what we want."

"That sounds nice, but it doesn't change anything for me," she answered with a mirthless laugh. Feng pushed herself out of the chair, grateful that Stephen didn't judge her for her weakness. "Well, enough of that. I'll go get more fully dressed and then meet you in your suite for the interrogation."

"You don't have to. I can do it without you."

"What? Why?"

"You know why, Feng. Look, you've been through a lot. I never even wanted you to go through the strain of this operation in the first place. I'll send June over to help you get ready for us to leave."

"Thank you, Stephen, but I won't make you do it on your own."

"With all due respect, I know you're a badass. But you're in no state of mind to do this. Besides, I've got someone else helping me."

"Who?"

"A friend of mine that came in from the States. He's kind of a…consultant."

"You have some pretty wild friends, Stephen. But I guess I have to trust you to be right."

Stephen smiled at her, sadly, before heaving Colin's immobilized body over his shoulder and carrying him out. Feng stared after them as Colin left her life again. When the door shut behind them, she finally allowed herself to break down and the tears to flow.

Colin fought against the weight of his eyelids and the fuzziness in his brain. He wasn't sure how a delicate creature like Feng was able to tackle him and knock him out, but she'd certainly managed it.

When he finally focused on the unfamiliar room around him, he looked around frantically, trying to find Feng. Dread crept into his stomach when all he saw was Stephen and another man he didn't recognize.

The contents of his bag were scattered around them as Stephen's dark-haired compatriot was feverishly typing away on a laptop, his brow furrowed in concentration. His rolled-up shirtsleeves revealed tattoos running up and down his forearms, with some markings also adorning a few of the fingers quickly clacking away at the keys.

"Oh good, you're up," Stephen said, patiently, walking over to him. He pulled a chair in front of Colin, taking a seat and resting his elbows on his knees.

It was unnerving how unfazed he seemed to be for a man whose girlfriend had spent much of the night with another man. Colin tried to move, only to discover he had a brutal headache and he was secured to his chair with some kind of restraints he couldn't identify.

"Take it easy, man," Stephen said, calmly. "Feng put you in a mean sleeper hold. Your head is probably killing you."

"What? Where is she? Is she okay?"

"She's fine. Hurt and disappointed by what you did, though she'd never admit it."

Colin swallowed hard in response, unable to formulate a coherent thought. Nothing about what was going on made any sense.

"I don't know what the fuck is going on, but if you want to try and beat the shit out of me, go ahead and get it over with. As long as you let me talk to Feng afterward."

The dark-haired guy working on the computer laughed out loud.

"What's *your* problem?" Colin demanded to him.

"Nothing," the stranger answered, still chuckling as he proceeded to return his eyes to the screen.

"You're confused, I get it," Stephen said, looking back at Colin. "Let's start over. That guy with all the tattoos over there is Trey Adler. He's busy trying to sort through what the hell you were trying to pull tonight. And I'm Stephen…Feng's handler."

"Handler? Feng's an agent? What the hell? CIA? NSA?"

"Technically we are CIA, but I prefer to think of us as a task force."

"Right. I bet you're just some kind of America-to-Asia outreach program," Colin sneered out. He'd been working on Lexis's team long enough to feel pretty hostile toward U.S. agents, but thinking that Feng was in harm's way on a regular basis for them made his blood boil.

"We're the good guys. Unlike the group you provide *your*…services to."

"You put Feng in danger every day she works with you. That doesn't make you a good guy as far as I'm concerned."

"No, Colin, you put her in danger by caring for her and getting into bed, literally and figuratively, with a bitter and twisted monster like Lexis. When Feng went to America looking for you…and almost found you, she caught our attention." Stephen paused to smile slightly, adding, "She's really amazing."

Colin's eyes narrowed. "Yes, she's incredible, and you need to remember she's mine, even if…"

"You can't be together, blah, blah, blah. Feng went over all this with me. Are you sure you aren't Chinese, Colin?" Stephen asked with a smirk.

Hatred, rage, and futile jealousy were swirling around inside Colin, but he could do nothing.

"We've been watching Lexis's team, and your involvement with it since you joined. Your name only popped up once or twice. We could never get enough evidence to prove it, but we were pretty sure what your role was. That's what gave our crew the idea to recruit Feng to help us as a foreign operative. Your feelings for each other were very appealing to my boss."

"You son of a bitch!"

"Calm down. I would never let anything happen to her. That's why I was chosen as her handler."

"But, why would she agree to work with you? She's Chinese. If her government knew…" Just the thought of what the Chinese government would do to her if they found out she was helping the U.S. with anything made Colin want to rip Stephen's arms off his body.

"I know she's Chinese, and she is also still in love with you. She agreed to assist us if we didn't hurt you."

"She did it for me?" he whispered, the words coming out remorseful and confused.

"Yes. Then she realized how great she is at helping America, especially when she saw what these dangerous criminals were doing all around the world. Not every operative, on the books or not, is American, even you know that, Colin."

Trying to wrap his head around it all, he finally asked, "But she's a pop singer. She's in the media all the time."

"We helped her with that. When we were setting up her cover, we quickly learned how talented she is. It's perfect. She can travel to almost every corner of the world without suspicion. Her Asian popularity is particularly helpful."

"Why did you come after me now?"

"We let you stay on the back burner like Feng wanted, but your projects have escalated and you were a bit too careless on that Sydney job."

Colin cringed at the memory. That one had been a disaster. The husband came home and set his eyes on Colin with his wife. He'd barely made it out, but Lexis said not to worry. She insisted there had been no fallout.

"I don't hurt anyone. I only get someone's name if they're with the people at least as bad as we are."

"You're still trying to convince yourself of that?" the guy named Trey finally asked, walking over with a file in his hand. "Maybe your role in all of this is mild, but what do you think happens with that information you get? You think Lexis just sells it, you all get rich, and no one gets hurt?"

Trey opened the file, showing him a picture of his Sydney target and her husband — both dead.

"You remember them, don't you?" Trey asked. "How about these people?" The tattooed bastard forced him to look at one picture after another, all of them showing some violent aftermath to his actions. "You must have suspected this happened, Colin, otherwise you wouldn't have tried to protect Feng."

"What do you mean?" he asked, his voice sounding unbelievable even to his own ears.

"We've been going through everything in your bag, including the very limited copy you'd made of Stephen's hard drive and what you left behind," Trey answered, pacing in front of him. "You destroyed or erased everything even mentioning Feng, and eliminated any ability to find Stephen or damage him, either. Burning the documents in the bathroom was ballsy, with Feng so close by, you know."

"I couldn't let that information get back to Lexis. From me, or anyone."

"That's very kind of you, even if we did make up all that data..." Trey stated.

"All of it?"

"Yes," Stephen answered. "It wasn't easy, either. I haven't been face forward on a mission for a few years now. I've spent my whole life in America, and I'm a U.S. citizen, but my family is Chinese. So I at least look the part of an ass-hat Chinese-American boyfriend with lots of money and secrets we knew Lexis wouldn't be able to resist pursuing."

"All that to catch me stealing information to prove I'm on Lexis's team?"

"Not really. Even if Feng wouldn't believe it, we were pretty sure. No, we had to see *what* you'd take when you got back here. Feng wasn't a part of that element of the plan. She'll probably be pissed at me about that. Either way, whether it was a setup or not, doesn't change that you showed us you were trying to shield Feng. Isn't that true?"

"Yes. I was going to give Lexis fake information and the dead end crap I did copy from the suite."

"Did it occur to you what Lexis would do if she figured it out?" Stephen asked.

"I assumed I'd be like those poor assholes in the pictures you two just showed me — dead. But I was going to make sure Feng would be long gone by then."

"That would explain the plane ticket along with the fake

passport you have with Feng's picture on it?"

"Yes. But it doesn't matter anymore. It's all over for me anyway. After all of this, Lexis will never let her go. She hates to lose. And as long as Feng's working with you, she'll always be in danger. I'll never be able to keep her safe."

"Oh, don't be so negative," Trey said, with a smile.

"What?" Colin lifted up his gaze to look at them.

"Why do you think we let you be alone with her?" Stephen asked. "We actually believe you have quite a bit of value, Colin. But we have to be honest with us — how far are you ready to go to get to be with Feng?"

"As far as it takes… Whatever it takes," Colin answered firmly.

"Good," Stephen said, seriously, before pushing a button on the desk next to them. He turned his face to the small speaker and asked, "Feng? Did you hear all that?"

Her voice came through the speaker, thick with emotion, and with one word she restored every ounce of hope Colin believed had been forever lost.

"Yes," she answered.

EPILOGUE

Feng turned her body in Colin's lap and placed her cold hands against his cheeks and kissed him. She let his warm breath enter her body. Her tongue stroked against his, desperately trying to taste him one more time, before he had to leave her again.

Breaking away from her lips, Colin rested his forehead on hers and sighed.

"I have to go soon," he whispered.

"I know. Colin, I hate this. It's too dangerous. Lexis has to suspect something. And I hate to think of you with those women."

"I've not had sex with any of them since, if that helps. I can go through with Stephen's plan for the most part, but now that I've had you in my arms again, I can't do that."

"That just makes it more likely that Lexis will figure out what you're doing. It was bad enough you had to give him all that dirt on her, *and* dig up information from your old assignments…"

Colin tilted her face up to meet his, making her eyes meet his own.

"Feng, we've got this. Lexis doesn't suspect anything and I've still managed to get all the information I need for my new assignments. I have to be more imaginative and charming, is all. And when I'm done, I just happen to give everything to Stephen, as well as Lexis. Nothing to be worried about."

"You're a terrible liar, Colin."

"Only with you. I'm pretty awful without you," he added, his green eyes darkening with heavy worry.

She kissed him again, until his arms snaked around her waist, and together they let go of some of the immense tension in their bodies.

A knock on the door shocked them to attention. Feng grabbed her handgun from the nightstand and Colin moved to place his body in front of hers.

"It's me, Stephen," they heard through the door, and Feng relaxed slightly. Stephen had arranged for this meeting. Rain was steadily streaking across the windows of the tiny boarding house in Ha Long Bay, Vietnam, where they were posing as tourists. Despite breathtaking views of the area's legendary and seemingly endless limestone monolithic islands, she and Colin had barely ventured outside once. He had barely a day to be with her, and to debrief Stephen on his last two assignments; making every second she had with him that much more precious.

It hadn't been long since they created this arrangement and the tiny stolen moments with Colin were amazing. But it didn't change how much she hated the risks he was taking — all for the chance that he'd do enough to help the U.S. government to take down Lexis's team.

This was their only chance at finally being free and together, but it was one helluva long shot.

Feng opened the door to Stephen, overcome with sadness at the knowledge this meant her time with Colin was coming to an end.

"Come in, Stephen. I guess it's time for us to get moving again?" Feng asked.

"It is, but shit just got a lot more urgent."

"Why? What happened?" Colin asked.

"It's Trey. He's missing."

TO BE CONTINUED...

THANK YOU FOR READING

Please keep reading for excerpts of THREE RIVERS, CITY OF CHAMPIONS and a sneak peek of A STEEL TOWN.

SHANGHAI WIND SOUNDTRACK

- ❖ *I Will Wait* — Mumford & Sons
- ❖ *She's Like The Wind* — Patrick Swayze
- ❖ *Let Her Go* — Passenger
- ❖ *You* — 1975
- ❖ *Baby Did A Bad, Bad Thing* — Chris Isaak
- ❖ *Hua Xie Liao (Withered Flower)* — Wong Fei
- ❖ *Thousand Miles* — Tove Lo
- ❖ *Jiang Ai (To Love)* — Wong Fei
- ❖ *Chandelier* — Sia
- ❖ *From Eden* — Hozier
- ❖ *Time Go* — Caught a Ghost
- ❖ *Pompeii* — Bastille
- ❖ *Divisionary (Do The Right Thing)* — Ages and Ages
- ❖ *Yu Tian (Rain)* — Sun Yan-zi
- ❖ *Collide* — Howie Day

Follow Chloe on Spotify to hear this and other soundtracks from future novels: http://open.spotify.com/user/chloetbarlow

I hope you get a chance to enjoy the rest of the Gateway to Love series:

ACKNOWLEDGMENTS

It's been almost a year since the release of my debut novel, *Three Rivers*, and my head is still spinning. I couldn't do any of this without the support of so many bloggers, reviewers, and readers like you. I would also like to thank some specific people for their help.

Once again, my sweet husband: Thank you for your patience, kindness, understanding, and your unending ability to instill me with romantic ideas.

My Agent: *Michelle Grajkowski* of *Three Seas Literary Agency* continues to support me and encourage me through this crazy world of publishing. I am so lucky to have met her.

Glorya Hidalgo: Thank you for believing in me from the beginning. To be included in an amazing anthology like *Pink Shades of Words* is truly an honor. I look forward to seeing you again at your great event *Authors in the OC!*

My Team: *Eisley Jacobs* of *Complete Pixels* always makes my vision an even better reality. She is an amazing graphic designer and person.

Marilyn Medina of *Eagle Eye Reads Editing*, what a relief it is to know that you will be there to whip my books into shape.

Kristina Ohrberg, and *Ashley Lake* you are my rocks. I

can't imagine trying to do with this without your assistance.

Consultants: Thank you *Linda Eng Reed* and *Marlena Salinas* for being my sounding boards on the cultural aspects of this story.

Also thank you to *Jewel Eng* and her mom is *Wendy Lim* for helping me with such beautiful artwork for this novella. Colin and Feng would love these images!

My Beta Readers and Author Mentors: Thank you so much to *Kristina Ohrberg, Ashley Lake, Linda Eng Reed,* and *Megan Kern.* I loved getting to share this story with you while it was still hot off the presses.

Chloe's Crew: Thank you again for all you do every day. Each of you is like family to me, and I couldn't be happier to call you my friends.

My Readers: Finally, it is with great pleasure that I thank each of my readers for enjoying the worlds I create. You are what make this all possible.

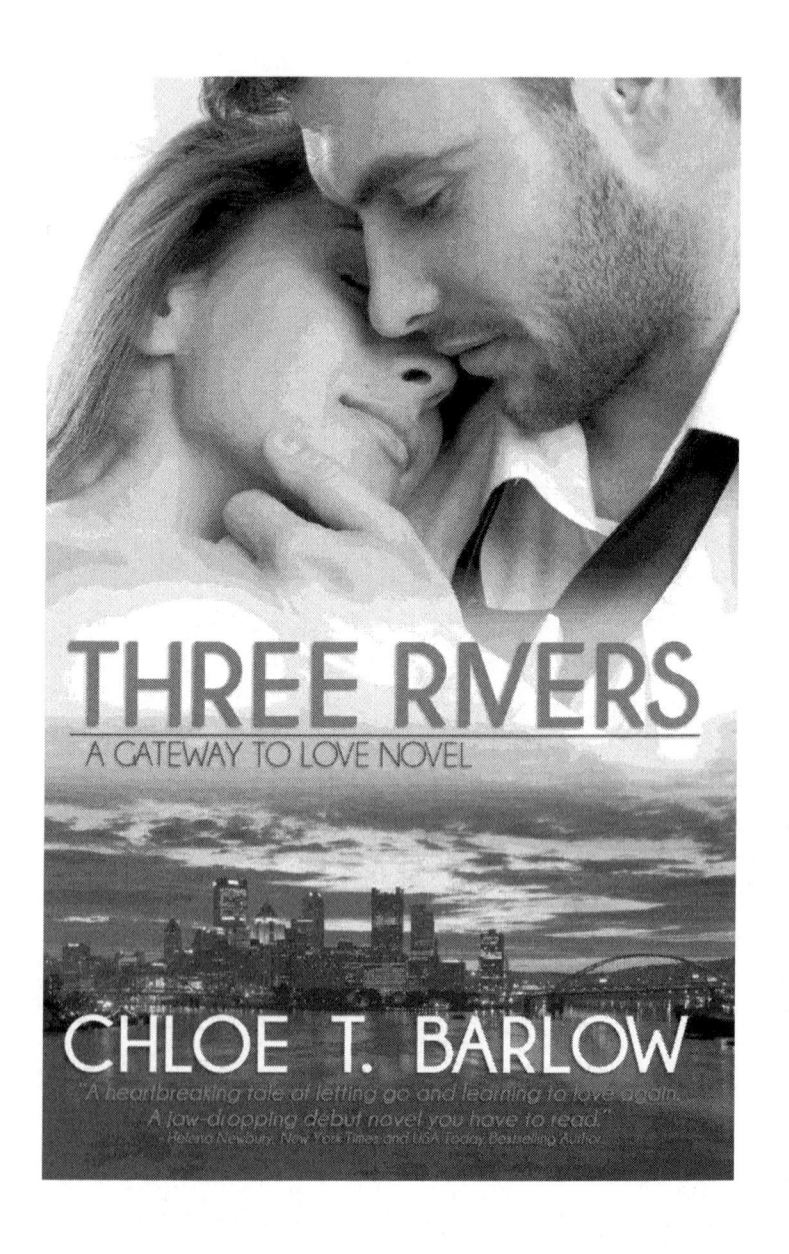

THREE RIVERS

A GATEWAY TO LOVE NOVEL

CHLOE T. BARLOW

"A heartbreaking tale of letting go and learning to love again.
A jaw-dropping debut novel you have to read."
Helena Newbury, New York Times and USA Today Bestselling Author

THREE RIVERS
BOOK ONE - A GATEWAY TO LOVE

How do you start over when you gave everything to one life, one plan, and lost it all?

Althea refuses to allow herself to love again. Imprisoned in grief at 24 after her husband's sudden death, she's convinced her heart died along with him. She spends her days honoring his memory by clinging to the legal career he helped her to build and to the remaining pieces linking them together.

Griffen's been running from his past. Despite success as an author and investigative journalist, he's been traveling through life on autopilot. For a decade, he's chosen perilous adventures and meaningless sex over the danger of any attachments. When he finally returns home to Pittsburgh, he's slammed by the awakened memories and regret he's spent years trying to escape.

A chance encounter brings them together. Their instant desire for each other – and the bond they discover between them – shocks them both. Despite her best efforts, Althea can't resist Griffen's charm or his intriguing proposition – if she agrees to a no-strings affair with him for the two weeks he's in town, he swears he'll walk away when their time is up. Assured she can test the waters of a new life while keeping her vow never to betray her husband's memory by opening her heart to another, Althea throws herself into the escape Griffen provides her.

Their perfect plans go awry when the intensity of their connection overwhelms them. Will they risk it all on the chance of something great together…or will the power of their secrets and guilt tear them apart?

THREE RIVERS EXCERPT

As he waited for his next drink, Griffen was finally feeling nicely buzzed and leaned back to observe the crowd, surprised by the hip cocktails and hipper clientele. Chic or stodgy, he didn't give a crap, but this certainly differed from the dive joints he remembered getting loaded in growing up. Several women gave him long, meaningful glances. He smirked back but couldn't get himself interested in that kind of distraction.

Before he could get too wrapped up in the same cycle of guilty thoughts, a lilting female laugh behind Griffen's back jarred him to attention.

After a heartier laugh followed, a throaty but feminine voice said, "Jeez ladies, I think he's a bit too hipster for me. If I hooked up with him, it would have to be done *ironically*. I mean, he's got a beard *and* he's wearing a vest!" Griffen laughed as the bartender put down his drink and he tried to listen in as inconspicuously as possible.

"What about that one?" Griffen heard a louder voice ask. "*Mmm*, what a fine ass, and nice broad shoulders. He's turning around...*come on lucky seven*. Uh-oh, no," she added with a snort. "Sorry Tea, my bad. He's got a hot body, but his face, blech. Moving on."

A third female voice said, "Excellent point. Let's keep looking in a logical manner. I'm not giving up yet. Hmm. He's too big, he's too young, he's too short, he's too...Ugh."

"All right Goldi*cocks*, I think you both have had your shot here. This is the third bar you've dragged me to tonight. It's late, my feet hurt and I think I've been a good sport. Let's move it along now, shall we? How about we just go home?

You promised me ice cream and pajamas if this didn't work out — I think it's time."

Aw hell no, Griffen thought, he had to get a look at this woman with the sexy voice before she left. He slowly turned around in his stool and his breath caught and his throat closed right around it. She was fucking gorgeous.

Her friends — Goldicocks one and two he presumed — flanked her. They were lovely in their own right, a blonde and a brunette, but he only had eyes for the honey haired beauty in front of him.

He looked down at his drink pretending not to hear them, when the brunette blurted, "Over there by himself at the bar in the gray sports jacket. Ooh, he's delicious. This Goldicocks says he's *just right*."

Griffen stifled a smile when he glanced at the sleeve of his gray sports jacket. *Oh yes, Goldicock number one, do me a solid with your friend please*, he silently pleaded.

"Uh, girls," the goddess stammered, "a little too perfect, don't you think? Not sure I can afford the stud fee on that one."

Griffen almost choked on his drink as he thanked God that women with a couple drinks in them lost all capacity to whisper effectively.

This pretty little thing finds me perfect, huh? Very far from the truth, but I can let her believe it for now. Maybe this night isn't a total loss after all.

He surreptitiously shifted in his stool so he could take her in more fully.

Gorgeous. That was the only word that kept going through his head. The only word he could say about her. He hadn't wanted any of the other women staring at him from around the bar, but this one was another thing altogether. She looked like exactly what he needed to take the edge off his internal shit storm. He had to have her.

Her hair was long and fell in waves across smooth, lovely shoulders and round, soft breasts that looked like they would fit nicely in his hands — and his mouth, which watered at the thought. It was her eyes that had him transfixed, though. They were wide and almond shaped and the most unique color — hazel, with radiating shades of gold and green throughout, with an outline of jet black around the irises making the unique color even more pronounced.

He stood up and walked toward her. She quickly realized what he was doing and her eyes suddenly turned scared and her cherry red lips parted slightly. She looked like a cornered deer recognizing a predator's scent in the air, but her eyes never drifted from each of his. They were like a tractor beam and he couldn't even feel his legs moving as he walked toward her.

"Hello, I couldn't help but overhearing that you're disappointed in tonight's offerings. I hope you aren't really leaving." She was sitting on a stool, so Griffen could look down at her without releasing her from his gaze.

From behind him he heard her two friends stumble out a flurry of assurances.

"Oh no, we're not leaving. Actually, Jenna and I just saw a friend of ours, right?"

"That's right, Brey, there is that friend over there. Hey...you." Griffen watched as his lovely conquest followed their retreating figures with wide eyes and visibly tensed up.

"Hi," she gulped out, training those beautiful eyes back on his. "No, I guess it looks like I'm not going anywhere for a while."

"Thank God, gorgeous," he drawled at her.

"Uh, what did you call me?" she asked on a gasp, sitting upright quickly.

"What? Oh, I called you gorgeous." He took advantage of her surprise to take her in more slowly. She was remarkably beautiful in a very unique way. Besides the hypnotic eyes that were doing some kind of Jedi mind trick on him, she had the fullest bottom lip with a perfect Cupid's bow on top. Everything about her was a combination of strong and soft — firm legs that were still softly sexy and shapely, a small waist and taut stomach that led up to smooth shoulders and pert rounded breasts.

She was stunning, yes, but what was truly knocking him off course was that although he'd never met her before, something about her seemed so familiar, but also so sad and a little lost. He alternately felt like kissing her senseless and just holding her on the sofa to watch a movie. Griffen had to shake himself back into the present.

Don't scare her man. You've been staring at her eyes and lips for possibly a creepily long amount of time. Get with it.

"Right." He cleared his throat. "I called you gorgeous and since I don't know your real name yet, I will just have to go with that for now, I guess. Unless you want to share that information with me?"

She seemed completely flustered at the endearment, which was adorable but befuddling.

Could she really not know how hot she is?

He leaned in close to her so she breathed the same air as him and he could tell it was setting her off balance.

"Althea," she whispered huskily, looking at him then quickly averting her eyes again. "You can call me Althea."

Holy hell, Althea thought, *this guy is way sexier than is even fair.*

She'd already been totally thrown by his looks, and then he called her gorgeous...she hadn't heard that nickname since Jack and it added to the way this whole experience was sending her neurons into overdrive. She blamed that for the confusing fact that she told him to call her Althea, instead of Tea.

She'd even blinked a couple of times as the name slipped out, seeing as she even used "Tea" professionally. It never felt like *Althea* really fit her. Apparently most people agreed, because no one ever called her that.

For as long as she could remember everyone shortened her name to Tea, or called her by her childhood nickname of "Sweet Tea," because she had always been such a *doggone* nice little thing.

Ironically, she'd been named after her man-eating great-grandmother who'd lived it up in Charleston, South Carolina in the roaring 20's with multiple husbands (some of whom died in mysteriously gothic southern ways).

Althea hadn't felt much like that kind of a vixen in, well, ever. No, that had never been her. She was respectable *Sweet Tea,* after all.

But there was something about the way Griffen stared into her eyes that made her heart stop and had her feeling at once at ease, yet also full of desire. She felt more intense, more daring, more connected to the wild woman that was her namesake.

"I'm Griffen. I would introduce myself to your friends, but it seems they had to be somewhere other than here very quickly." He grinned, revealing two of the sexiest, deepest dimples she'd ever seen. Althea had a sudden desire to dig her nose into one of those cute things and wiggle it around, until she realized she was staring and couldn't help but feel a blush spread across her cheeks.

"Yes, they do seem to have run off, haven't they? I guess it's just you and me," she responded as she tried to turn her head and stop staring at him, but she was pretty sure she just looked like she had some kind of a facial tic.

"That works for me," he said with a twinkle in his eye.

Althea had really just been humoring the girls. She'd never actually intended to hook up with anyone. The plan was to have a few drinks and laughs with her friends, maybe look at some guys, flirt with one or two. Those had been the baby steps she'd really had in mind. Yet Griffen was so exciting and new, while at the same time something about him seemed so natural, that she couldn't imagine doing anything that night except for enjoy spending time with him.

Only problem? She was sitting in front of him completely mute, her mind blank of anything to say, and it hit her — she was totally incapable of talking to men, especially this man, romantically. This would likely turn embarrassing fast and it didn't help that she was so damn twitchy. Now it was her leg that kept jumping up and down erratically.

"Do I make you nervous?" he asked.

"A little," she muttered in a voice she barely recognized.

"Just breathe," he whispered. Althea blew out a huge gust of air.

"Thanks," she said, feeling embarrassed.

"I can't have you pass out on me."

"Sorry, I'm a little out of practice at this."

"At what? Talking to a handsome stranger in a bar? I think you're doing just fine."

"Well, you think highly of yourself, don't you?" she said with a smirk and she noticed his eyes drop to her mouth again.

"Don't you?"

"Think highly of *myself*?" Althea asked confused.

"No," he teased and then let half his mouth turn up in what might have been a smirk or was more likely some precursor to his wolfish plan of eating poor Little Red Riding Althea whole. "Of *me*."

"Puh-leeze," she groaned with an epic roll of her eyes. "You *can't* be serious."

"I'm not, but I did make you forget how nervous you are with me for a moment, didn't I?"

She couldn't lie, it had, but she didn't want to give him too much credit. "You certainly made for a good distraction, I will give you that. Thank you."

Though he'd only helped to distract her from her nervousness. Other than that she was hyper-focused — on him: his impossibly aqua blue eyes (s*eriously, is that even a real eye color?*); his broad shoulders; that delicious mouth; the way his slightly shaggy hair grazed his dark brows. Everything about him was hardwired to excite her on every level. Even the one inch vertical scar next to his left eyebrow, that was the only thing marring the perfection of his masculine beauty, drove her insane. Althea wondered if it would be rude to lick that scar in front of a bar full of strangers...?

She couldn't believe she was thinking this way about a man after all these years, but it was as though he'd been crafted and chiseled to make her do something crazy and she liked the feeling.

"Let's go back to the basics. How about that?"

"The basics?"

"Yeah, the basics. I know your name's Althea. Next up —

where are you from?"

"Charlotte, North Carolina."

"Dogs or cats?"

"Huh?"

"Do you prefer dogs or cats?" he repeated slowly with a smirk.

"I'm just a general animal lover..."

"Bullshit."

She gasped.

"Everyone has a preference, spill it."

"Okay," she laughed. "Dogs."

"Good answer. Do you cry at those emotionally manipulative Sarah McLachlan commercials about animal cruelty?"

"Of course! You?"

"Maybe..."

"Maybe?"

"All right, definitely, and I always donate a ton of money every time. I think I've ended up with five subscriptions to their magazine by now. Okay. Back to you. Birthday?"

"June 15."

"See how easy this is? Good, now ask me something."

Althea's mouth suddenly went dry and her palms were sweating. She knew that if she put her hand on the bar, she would leave a steamy handprint behind.

Gross, she thought. *Jesus Althea, come on. Ask him something, anything. Baby steps or not, could you be more boring? IRS agents sound more exciting than you. Maybe you should offer to do his taxes, that'll make his night. At least ask him a question. You're so wound up you've got this guy asking enough about you to fill out a visa application for you to go to Abu Dhabi. Least you could do is ask him something back!*

She was having some sort of flirtation stage fright and it

was kind of humiliating. She tried desperately to remember how to do this but God she hadn't really flirted with anyone since flip phones were an exciting technological development. She looked down and glanced up at Griffen through her lashes, feeling incredibly self-conscious and for some reason — like a failure.

She couldn't believe how much she really wanted something to happen with Griffen. They had steamy glances back and forth down but she would have to talk more or they would start looking like they belonged on a show on *The WB* when what she was really feeling about this guy was more in line with late night on *Skinemax*.

Althea felt way out of her league but kept reminding herself:

This is just a baby step — I can do this.

Ha, she thought, *this guy is no baby step, he is a full marathon of hotness, an Olympic long jump of yumminess.*

Maybe I can still go after that slightly chubby hipster. Is he still here? He seems a better way to get back into things. I mean, he may want to discuss his kitschy collection of ceramic diner milk servers, but I can deal with that. I can't deal with someone this irresistible. At least not yet, right?

"Hey, are you still breathing over there?" Griffen asked, stroking his fingers over her hand and resting two on her pulse with a smirk. Althea hadn't realized so much time had passed but his touch burned the delicate skin on her wrist, jolting her very much to the present.

"Oh, sorry, I was just thinking."

"About what?"

"You," she said, barely above a whisper.

"Good," he leaned closer and looked in her eyes. "I like you thinking about me, then I don't feel so alone in the fact that I'm sure I won't stop thinking about you for a while." His eyes darted down to her lips and she wondered if he may kiss her. Instead his eyes looked uncertain for a moment and then he leaned back and picked up her drink. He tasted it and let his tongue dart to pick up a drop that lingered on his bitable bottom lip. "Mmm, a manhattan?"

"Ye-es, they age it in oak barrels for months to develop the flavor. It's my favorite drink." Althea's voice sounded thick and husky to her ears.

"Is that so? Well, then you should be enjoying it more, shame to let something so perfectly developed go to waste." Griffen looked down her body then back up to her lips and leaned the glass to them. As he tilted it up, she opened her mouth to swallow the smooth but heady cocktail. Griffen replaced the glass on the bar and moved his rough thumb across the swell of her lower lip to collect some of the drink that remained there. Althea gasped slightly. His thumb was delightfully cool, but she felt like her lip was on fire. Without looking away from Althea's eyes, Griffen placed his thumb gently into her mouth. "Don't want to miss this, do we?"

Althea looked back at him and sucked his thumb into her mouth. His eyes widened, clearly shocked at how bold she'd so quickly become, but he smiled in glee as soon as he recovered, dimples in full effect. Althea smiled back and let her bottom teeth scrape the pad of his thumb while she sucked at him with her greedy mouth.

"Althea..." Griffen removed his thumb on a slow groan of her name.

She was so glad she told him her whole name now. Just hearing those syllables on his tongue had her warm all over and embarrassingly wet between her legs, because in that moment he made her feel so sexy.

It thrilled her to think that for just one night she could be someone else — not a boring mom or a lonely widow, but a glamorous, desirable woman who could hold her own with a delectable man such as Griffen. The thought that she could turn him inside out, make *him* want *her*, was more intoxicating than the strong cocktail in her hand.

"So, what do you do?" she squeaked loudly, suddenly overcome by how quickly everything was getting away from her and by the pleasantly warm and thrilling sensation running through her from his touch.

If the rest of him tastes as good as that thumb I need to stop being an idiot and make at least something happen tonight. She grabbed her manhattan from the bar and took a big gulp of it. *Let's do this girl,* she cheered to herself.

Griffen laughed at how the woman in front of him so quickly switched from Jessica Rabbit to Jessica Fletcher, as he quickly gestured for the bartender to come over.

"Another round, man? It's last call."

Griffen nodded and watched his new best friend rush away to make their drinks, as his mind went back to how charming and unpretentious Althea was.

She smiled at him with that sexy half smile of hers and his heart clenched again as she asked, "You know, what do you do — what is your day job? Since I can only assume you spend your nights interrogating other helpless women like myself." She gave Griffen a little raised eyebrow and a smirk and it hit him straight in his crotch. She was starting to open up and he could tell this was just going to get more fun.

"I'm shocked, just *shocked* that you think so poorly of me. You're the only woman I'm interested in interrogating right now, nighttime or not, but as for how I spend my time when I'm not trying to monopolize yours...I'm in town for a couple weeks as a visiting professor at Pitt. Journalism and nonfiction writing."

Okay, it's true for now, he thought to himself.

He didn't want to give her any indication that he was rolling in it. It was refreshing to be around a woman that didn't know who he was or what he had, and he wanted to keep it that way.

"Pitt, really? What a coincidence."

"Christ you aren't a Pitt student are you? Because picking up a Pitt student would *not* be the way to start off on the right foot," he laughed. "Even if it is just a short visit."

"Oh no!" she laughed. "Pitt Law School. Class of '08."

"So, this one's pretty obvious then, but I'll ask anyway. What do *you* do?"

"I'm a lawyer," she grinned.

"You don't say," he said sarcastically. "All right, now, what kind of lawyer are you?"

"I do complex commercial litigation."

"Big firm, little firm?"

"Big global monster firm."

"Exciting?"

"Not really." He quirked an eyebrow at her.

"Everyone pictures Boston Legal," she looked at his slightly confused face and added, "or whatever show about lawyers people are watching these days...but it's really one big company fighting another big company. I get into court and I find it interesting, so it works for me."

When the fresh cocktails arrived they held them up to each

other. "What should we drink to?" Griffen asked.

"Baby steps," she said back to him.

"Not sure what that means, but works for me. To baby steps and a beautiful woman in a helluva dress." She wore a cherry red dress that was low-cut and gathered provocatively around her breasts. It hugged all her curves in a way that made his hands itch to do the same. The straps were thick and soft and sat just right on her enticing shoulders. He wanted to bite those shoulders — and soon.

"Oh, um, thanks," she said blushing.

Christ, that blush is beautiful, he thought. He couldn't think of the last time he'd even seen a woman blush.

"Well, it is *some* dress and you look great in it," he said, slowly perusing her red clad frame.

She rolled her eyes. "I would've preferred jeans and a brow-beater but the girls hijacked my clothes too."

"Brow-beater?"

"Calling a ribbed tank top a 'wife beater' is misogynistic — so I say 'brow beater.'"

He laughed. "I never thought of it that way, you're full of surprises."

She winced, "Oh God."

"What?"

"I just realized how bad I am at this. I mean here is this great looking guy talking to me and I can't stop blathering on about stupid stuff like tank tops."

He leaned forward and whispered, "I think you're doing great, gorgeous."

"Yeah, swimmingly," she muttered sarcastically.

"Let me guess. You're not used to this?"

"Is it that obvious?"

"A little. But it's sweet. Adorable."

"Yup. Every girl's dream. Meet a handsome stranger and he thinks she acts like a newborn deer wobbling all over the place."

"I didn't know newborn deer were sexy as hell. Because trust me, Althea, you are."

"Oh. Thanks," she managed to breathe out.

Griffen laughed despite himself and his seemingly never-ending supply of lustful thoughts. The sound was almost foreign to his own ears. He hadn't had much reason to laugh for a long time.

"And trust me, you couldn't do anything to make me not want to rip your clothes off."

"What?" she shrieked.

"Don't get me wrong, you're funny, brilliant and completely charming. Add on that you're beautiful and sexy as hell and I'm pretty much at your mercy right now," he smirked. "I'm wondering if I should be worried about the power you have over me."

"Really? Ah, no, I'm a sweetheart."

"I'll hold you to that, Althea. In fact," he said, placing a hand at her lower back until she gasped, "I would like to hold you to a lot of things."

"Ooh, that's a good line."

"A line?" he asked, his hand leaving her back to rest on his chest, his brow furrowing in a perfect image of false hurt. "You wound me, gorgeous."

"I'm sure your ego will recover."

"I'm not sure, I may need a bit of special attention, just to be sure." She rolled her eyes at him again and he simply smirked right back at her.

"All right, another question. Favorite movie?" he asked.

"Chinatown."

"Come on, *actual* favorite movie, not what you tell people to sound deep."

She giggled. "Legally Blonde."

"And the truth shall set her free," he teased. "Favorite song?"

"*In Your Eyes*, but only in *Say Anything*." He raised an eyebrow and she whispered, "I've always had an unhealthy crush on John Cusack."

"Hmm, now where am I going to find an enormous boom box in this century? Will it get you to come back to my hotel with me if I hold my iPhone over my head and play that song?" He started fiddling theatrically with the music controls on his iPhone.

She choked on her manhattan and almost spilled it down her front. "Go back with you?"

"Ooh, and I thought I slipped that in sneakily enough."

"I thought slipping it in was why you were trying to get me to go back with you," she blurted without thinking. "Oh my God, I just said that out loud. Can we go back to talking about tank tops please?"

"We can, but don't you think this is more interesting? I want you to leave with me tonight, Althea." He wasn't touching her but his nearness was driving her crazy. His lips were right next to her ear when he whispered, "Do *you* want to leave with me?"

"Oh. Well, um." She knew her eyes belied her growing terror and nervousness.

"Althea, I could give you a bunch of bogus reasons. Offer to show you the great view. To make you a signature cocktail or some other bullshit. But the truth is this bar is closing and I don't want to go to another one. I want to be alone with you. I'm just not ready to let you go. So will you come with me?"

He was leaning close to her ear, his breath spreading across her cheek and the warm air sent a rush of heat through her that had her body flushing and her heart racing. She wasn't ready to let him go, either.

The idea of being with him tonight suddenly seemed more than tempting — it was *necessary*.

No one had ever had this effect on her other than Jack. She knew she may never feel this way about someone again.

Can't I just let myself have this? Just one night with no strings. Let myself pretend to be someone else. Someone bold? Someone free?

Can I have just one night without fear and guilt, without crushing loneliness?

Before she knew what she was doing, Althea turned her head slightly so their cheeks touched, sending another rush of electricity straight to her core. The wait seemed to go on for an eternity but her mouth finally said, ever so softly, "Okay."

Griffen lowered his head next to her neck and breathed in deeply. "Thank you. So are you ready to go?"

She raised her head so she could look into his crystal blue eyes, so full of desire and said with more courage than she felt, "Yes. I just need to tell my friends." She looked around and met their gaze. She jerked her head to beckon them to her until their eyes widened and they ran over.

"So, I don't need a ride home," she whispered to them.

"Oh, gotcha," Aubrey smirked at her, then quickly turning toward Griffen with narrowed eyes she asked, "Is our girl safe with you? You aren't a serial killer, are you? Don't lie to me, I can sniff out a liar."

"No. She's completely safe with me."

"Hmm, that *is* what a serial killer would say, but you seem honest. Here, let me take your picture. If anything happens to her — you're toast," Aubrey snapped a shot, looked at it and said, "hmm, can't see your butt in this one. I'm gonna need you to stand up and turn around."

"Aubrey!" Althea interrupted. "I think that picture is more than enough. *Behave.*"

"All right, you know how to reach us," Jenna added. They kissed her cheeks and Jenna whispered in her ear so only she could hear, "You got this girl. We're proud of you and we're just a call away if you change your mind."

After they walked away, Althea turned and stared at Griffen, making no move toward her purse. He leaned closer to her and whispered, "Are you sure?"

"Yes, I'm really ready now." Althea looked at his outstretched hand and slid her long fingers across his palm and resting her hand in his. She licked her dry lips and looked up at him, thrusting up her chin in a dramatic show of confidence she only half felt. "Let's go."

As they walked out of the bar into the warm night air, Griffen placed a light hand to the small of her back and it awakened a world of nerve endings in her that had for too long been forgotten.

CITY OF
CHAMPIONS

A GATEWAY TO LOVE NOVEL

CHLOE T. BARLOW

CITY OF CHAMPIONS
BOOK TWO - A GATEWAY TO LOVE

How do you find the will to try, when you've spent all of your life playing on a field strewn with shattered lives and broken rules?

Tragedy and betrayal taught Jenna Sutherland early on that her safest bet was to fiercely avoid any risk, whether it is in work, life, or love. Now a respected orthopedic surgical resident on the cusp of finally breaking through in her career, she's more guarded than ever.

When injured NFL quarterback Wyatt McCoy bulldozes into her life there's no denying he's cocky, selfish, and downright dangerous — everything Jenna's sworn she doesn't want.

Suddenly the levelheaded doctor finds herself facing down her greatest fear, and she's tempted to gamble all she's fought so hard to build. The two embark on an intense holiday love affair that quickly teeters on obsession, and tempts them both to think they could go all-in on a real future together. Yet Wyatt's desperation to stay *on* the field — and *out* of the operating room — lures him to take dangerous risks with Jenna's trust.

Will they win at love or lose everything — *including their fragile chance at happiness?*

CITY OF CHAMPIONS EXCERPT

"Tea, I'm gonna head home and skip the tour," Jenna whispered to Tea as they followed Tom Wilkins, the assistant GM of the Pittsburgh Roughnecks, who was chattering almost nonstop several feet ahead of them to Griffen and Johnny.

"No way, Jenna," Tea whispered back more intensely, stopping suddenly until Aubrey barreled into her from behind.

"Jeez Tea, are you trying to kill me?" Aubrey huffed at her.

"No, but I may kill Jenna. She wants to go home," Tea turned back to Jenna with a surprising amount of frustration in her eyes, considering she was usually so sweet — maybe a little dramatic at times, but always sweet. "You really can't be serious, Jenna. Not after Griffen went to all this trouble setting up this day for us."

Jenna had to admit to herself that it was an impressive feat on Griffen's part. He'd used his connections with Tom, who was an old high school buddy of his and Tea's deceased husband, Jack's, to get them seats in the owners' box and now this private tour of the stadium facilities accompanied by a meet and greet with three starting players.

Any other day she'd be jumping at the chance, but after finding out the *University of Pittsburgh Medical Center's* fellowship in orthopedic sports medicine she so coveted was more out of reach than she realized and another depressing call with her dad, all she wanted to do was take a hot shower, eat ice cream, and hide — and not necessarily in that order.

"It was really sweet of him, Tea," Jenna said calmly, "and I do appreciate it, but I had a crappy day and am totally beat. I went to the game, hung out in the box with everyone, it's not like I blew this off."

"Jenna I can't believe you're missing a chance to check out some hot NFL players in the flesh — you know, when you aren't working and servicing them professionally," Aubrey said to Jenna, her voice dripping with its signature class and grace.

"Jesus Brey, why do you always make me being a sports medicine doc sound like I'm a hands-on sex therapist for athletes?"

"Because that would be a way more fun thing to hear you blather on about in our apartment instead of ACLs *this* and rotator cuffs *that*," Aubrey responded, closing her eyes, flopping her head to the side, and making distinct snoring sounds.

Jenna rolled her eyes at Tea but was getting no support from that member of their triad. Instead Tea simply glared at her.

"Hey, are you guys coming?" Jenna heard Griffen's deep voice boom back to them. He jogged in their direction and immediately looked at Tea with concern. "Gorgeous, is everything okay?" he asked her softly as he placed his hand at the small of her back. Tea looked up at him and the two simply stared in each other's eyes for a moment. The adoration they shared for each other was almost palpable. The moment was at once intimate and touching, making Jenna feel like a voyeur — a *very single* voyeur.

Ugh, now I'm feeling lonely on top of everything else, Jenna thought to herself as she made a mental catalog of the comfort foods presently in her apartment. *I'm going to need more ice cream, maybe I should stop on the way home.*

"I'm fine," Tea said reassuringly to Griffen. "It's Jenna, she's got a bad case of the stick-in-the-muds. She's trying to go home."

"No way, Jenna, this is a huge opportunity to meet these players and they're expecting all of us, it will look bad if one of us bails. It'll be short, I promise, and I know Johnny will be bummed if you leave...*Please*."

Griffen shot his best puppy dog eyes at her, bending his head down and letting his longish, dark wavy hair fall on his forehead.

"Uh oh, Jenna, he's got you in his blue-eyed clutches, you're toast," Aubrey said with a giggle, which Tea quickly joined in on with her own snickering.

Griffen wouldn't look away and threw out his bottom lip further. Jenna had to admit that he was devastatingly handsome. Yes, he was madly in love with her best friend but she was a woman, after all.

"Fine," Jenna muttered as she started walking toward Tom and Johnny.

"Success!" Griffen shouted with a fist pump in the air while Tea and Aubrey cheered. "Come on, hurry up ladies, they're waiting for us."

"All right folks, are we ready?" Tom asked when they caught up to him. Everyone nodded and proceeded to fall in behind him again like obedient ducklings until they made it to the entry area in the NFL team's locker room.

Tom stood next to the three players that were pegged for the meet-and-greet portion of what was rapidly feeling like one of the longest days of Jenna's life.

"I have our quarterback Wyatt, wide receiver JJ, and cornerback Trajan here to meet you. If you're NFL fans, as I know at least a couple of you are, they won't need much introduction," Tom said with a smooth tone suffused with authority.

Johnny's eyes were wide with excitement and Jenna stood amazed at how he was speechless for probably the first time since he was born. She loved to see Johnny so happy and proud, knowing that his "Gwiff" did all this for him.

She also noted that each of the three handsome players waiting for them had showered and seemed amiable enough, despite what was surely the annoying task of meeting "VIP Pittsburgher" Griffen Tate and his motley crew entourage after a long game and depressing defeat in overtime.

Jenna knew this was a unique opportunity for her to build on her growing relationship with the team as a potential go-to orthopedic surgeon, but it was hard to shake off her bad mood, especially when the notorious Wyatt Alejandro McCoy was eyeing her like she was a glistening Mojito on a hot day at the beach.

The son of a Mexican model and one of the greatest NFL quarterbacks of the 1980's, he was only in his second season with the Roughnecks, but had quickly developed the kind of reputation that a sensible woman like herself knew to steer clear of — even if he *was* blindingly good-looking.

She'd watched him like a hawk during the whole game, but assured herself that her acute interest was purely due to her love of the game and a small concern for what looked like a subtle issue with his throwing arm.

Yet, with each moment he stared at her, her blood warmed and her ability to ignore the focused gaze of his gray-green eyes became increasingly difficult.

"What do you say, guys?"

"Huh?" Jenna muttered inelegantly, completely oblivious to anything in the room but the arrogant grin on Wyatt's face.

Aubrey, who never missed a beat when it came to tormenting her friends, immediately pounced.

"Tom here asked if we wanted a tour. I was thinking maybe we should split up. Mr. McCoy, our friend Jenna here doesn't know much about football, could you possibly..."

"Take her on a private tour for more focused instruction?" he asked with that same damned leering expression.

"No, that's not necessary," Jenna responded curtly.

"I insist. It would be my pleasure. Though I didn't catch your name," Wyatt inquired.

"Jenna, her name's Jenna," Tea blurted out, knocking her forward with her shoulder. "And you two should definitely split off, what a great idea," Tea crooned with a devilish grin.

"Tea, jeez," Jenna whispered scowling at her. She couldn't believe that they were messing with her like this. Well, actually she could believe it. They all did it to each other, she just preferred to be on the giving end of it. "Sorry for the hold up guys, we just need to chat for a bit," Jenna said, dragging Tea and Aubrey out of earshot of the group of confused men.

"What the hell are you two up to?" Jenna whispered with irritation.

"What?" Tea whispered back innocently and then twisted her face into a scheming sneer. "Are you the only person that can torment her friends into talking to guys?"

Jenna turned to Tea and gave her a full scowl, "Seriously...notorious high profile athlete a-holes? You know the answer to that," Jenna whispered back. "I'll just go on the tour with you guys."

"Now Jenna, you wouldn't want to look rude after members of such an important part of your growing career have been so gracious to us, would you?" Aubrey teased.

"Dammit Aubrey," Jenna fumed.

"You know I'm right. Now stop being so pissy and let that hot guy show you around before you offend him or anyone else here." Aubrey responded calmly.

"Fine," she huffed, turning to face Wyatt. "All right Mr. McCoy, let's go," Jenna said, walking toward him with her toughest facial expression. It just seemed to make him more amused.

"Please call me Wyatt. How about we start with the locker room, that seems as good a place as any to begin your education," Wyatt drawled at her.

Of all the days to have to deal with a cocky self-impressed jackass...This guy can't be for real, Jenna thought to herself in frustration. *It's official, I will be killing Aubrey and Tea later. But I'm stuck with him now, so my double homicide plans will have to wait.*

Jenna took a steadying breath. She then steeled her nerves and schooled her face into its most confident expression before responding, "Sounds good Mr. McCoy."

"Oh come on, now. Don't be so formal. Don't you like me, sugar?"

"I just met you, I have no opinion of you," she answered.

"I don't think you're being honest. I think you definitely have an opinion of me, and it doesn't seem good," he responded, leading her into the expansive room lined with cherry wood lockers, benches, and various equipment. Jenna had been in countless locker rooms during her life — including this one — but the nearness of Wyatt McCoy made it feel surreal and claustrophobic.

It was a dream set-up for an athlete like herself, but all she could focus on was the singing heat coursing through her from merely his fingertips on her lower back.

She turned to him to break the connection, but that only served to plant her back against a locker and her face smack dab in front of his well-built chest.

Her sense of *déjà vu* was overwhelming — the feeling that she'd been in this place before and it had ended so very badly.

Jenna looked up into his eyes and immediately regretted it. Having spent so many years avoiding any romantic involvements with athletes, her instant attraction to this one was vexing to say the least.

Wyatt looked down at her and smiled. "Now that I have your attention, maybe we can get to know each other better, you can give me a chance to improve that low opinion you have of me. Did you like the game?"

"It was a tough loss and you seemed to be having a rough go of it."

"Ouch, that hurts."

"You keep telegraphing your throws like that and you're going to spend the rest of the season on your ass — trust me, that will hurt a lot more. You need to shorten your release," Jenna advised him.

"Um, I'm not sure I heard you right. What was that again, sugar?"

"Just critiquing your throwing style is all," she answered.

"So, you were watching me closely, sugar?"

"It's an occupational hazard."

He looked confused for a moment but quickly regained his cocky composure. Meanwhile, Jenna kept feeling hers slipping away from her.

With each unsteady breath she noticed another aspect of him that was intoxicating to her, whether it was the slight golden streaks in his chestnut hair, the matching hint of stubble on his strong jaw, or his broad shoulders — everywhere she rested her eyes on him only served to make her body more consumed with attraction and her brain more furious with that fact.

"Well, for the record, I've never heard any complaints about my release," he said with a wink and Jenna rolled her eyes in disgust, which only made him chuckle in amusement. "Though I thought you weren't supposed to know about football, sugar?"

"No. My *ex*-best friends were playing a joke. Now that you know the truth, I'll be moving along, let you get back to your life."

"But I'm having so much fun pretending to educate you. Maybe I can teach you Spanish."

"I already speak Spanish so you've got nothing to teach me."

"Oh I wouldn't be so sure of that. How about I teach you to relax?" he whispered in her ear — sending a shot of warmth coursing through her traitorous body.

"I'm plenty relaxed," she huffed. He smirked again, running a finger across her shoulder until she jumped.

"Relaxed, really? Hmm," he added with a cocky drawl and a slow perusal of her body that had her stomach tightening, even as her jaw clenched in irritation.

Wyatt leaned into her until she could smell his freshly washed hair and count the beads of water on the part of his skin bared by the undone buttons at the top of his crisp Italian shirt. He was insanely attractive and far too close for Jenna's comfort. She cringed a little at her own big mouth, wishing she'd left this bad boy well enough alone. The worst thing you can do with someone like Wyatt is to engage him, and she'd done worse, she'd *challenged* him.

Dammit Jenna, rookie mistake! she thought, chastising herself.

Jenna shook herself out of her hormonal stupor and stood up straight enough that he backed off a bit, "I have to ask—

does this usually work?"

"What do you mean, sugar?"

"I mean this ego the size of Texas routine of yours. The 'sugars' and the double entendres. I mean, come on. You want my opinion of you? Here it is. I find your little shtick — *and you* — exhausting and insulting. Please excuse me. I need to get back to my friends."

"I was under the impression my 'little shtick' was working," he teased, raising a hand and placing it alongside her head.

"Please. Working? Hardly," Jenna said, rolling her eyes again theatrically and ignoring the tightening in her belly and her intense desire to bury her face in his chest and just sniff him for a while.

Pull yourself together Jenna! she ordered to herself.

"Come on sugar, play nice," Wyatt said with a devious half-smile, looking down at her smugly.

"My name is not *sugar*, you jerk!" Jenna shouted and his laugh in response had her face red in anger and humiliation.

Right at that moment, the rest of her group walked in and Jenna felt sheer mortification at her position — pressed up against Wyatt McCoy of all people, in front of a locker — practically in her place of business — screaming at him.

Everyone looked at Jenna in shock at her outburst, though Aubrey merely looked thrilled at Jenna's current predicament.

"Don't worry folks, we're fine in here. I'll bring your friend to you soon."

"No, that won't be necessary, I can go now," Jenna said as calmly as she could muster. She smoothed down her shirt in an effort to regain control of herself. She was about to speak when she heard, "Hey Doc!"

Jenna looked up quickly, averting her eyes from her nosey companions and saw the kind face of one of her patients.

"Hi Eloni!" Jenna threw Wyatt a sharp look but he wouldn't move. He still had his hand placed on the wall next to her head and the fiery effect he had on her sex drive was quickly replaced with plain raw irritation.

That's more like it, she thought. *Best to remember why you stay away from these types of guys in the first place.*

She began to dart under his arm, but he only lowered it more.

"Doctor?" Wyatt asked with a cocked eyebrow.

"Yes, Mr. McCoy, they let us little ladies be doctors now. What a world! Now, if you would please move your arm."

"Hey Wyatt, how ya doin' man? How do you know Doctor S.?" Eloni asked with his usual gentle-giant charm. He was an offensive lineman from Samoa and a University of Hawaii graduate, and one of the first NFL players to give her a chance.

"Fine Eloni," Wyatt gritted out. "I was giving her a tour."

"Oh yeah? What brings you here Doctor S.? Visiting a patient?"

"No, I came with some friends." Jenna breathed more easily as she turned her attention away from the incredibly unsettling quarterback. "Griffen over there is buds with your assistant GM," she answered jerking a thumb over to her group that was now listening to a speech about on field safety. "How's the knee, Eloni?" She could feel Wyatt's eyes boring into the side of her face, but she refused to look in his direction.

"Well, my knee feels like a million bucks. You're a miracle worker Doctor S."

"It's all due to you and your hard work. Maybe they'll start naming the surgery after you, you keep playing so well..."

"Hey, Eloni, I think Coach is looking for you," Wyatt's voice boomed as he turned to his teammate. His nearness still overwhelmed Jenna and she started to make her escape.

"Well, Eloni, it was good to see you. I'm heading off, too," Jenna said and started walking toward her friends.

"Hey, where are you going?" Wyatt asked, walking alongside of her. "I wasn't done."

"I was."

"Oh come on. What are you doing tonight?"

"I have plans," she answered, nearing Tea and Aubrey, finally.

"No she doesn't," Aubrey blurted out.

"See, looks like you're all cleared to let me keep changing that opinion of yours about me. I won't even call you sugar, *Doc.*"

"No need," Jenna answered, throwing Aubrey a sharp look before shouting, "Hey Johnny, get over here." Johnny looked at Griffen and when he nodded Johnny ran over to her.

"Hey, Johnny, Wyatt here said he'd love to watch you throw."

"Awesome! Let's do it," Johnny said enthusiastically.

"That's great man, I appreciate it, too. Tom would that be okay?" Griffen asked his friend as he walked over.

"Of course. Come on Wyatt, let's do it on the field. You guys can come take pictures if you like," Tom added.

"Well, y'all have fun. I think I learned enough for one day," Jenna said as she stared in triumph at Wyatt.

He looked back at her with a challenge in his eyes and leaned down to whisper in her ear, "Have a nice night, but know that this ain't over, Doc."

A shiver ran down Jenna's spine as she watched six feet four inches of diabolically gorgeous trouble walk away from her and she struggled to decide whether she wanted to view his words as a threat — or a delicious promise.

A STEEL TOWN
BOOK THREE - A GATEWAY TO LOVE

Claudia McCoy has been told what she can't do enough for one lifetime. After a near-fatal childhood battle with juvenile diabetes and having to accept that her dreams of serving the military in combat would never come true, she's thrilled to begin a life on her own terms. Yet, when she finally starts her career in the FBI, Claudia is furious to discover her overbearing big brother, Wyatt, has once again stepped in where he wasn't wanted. His interference has derailed her from her high-profile aspirations of a position in the FBI's D.C. headquarters, planting her instead practically right into his Pittsburgh backyard.

Trey Adler is known for fixing things, but he's also broken just as many — leaving him with regrets that will never go away. He'd be the first to agree he should stay away from a nice girl like Claudia, but he can't deny his friend Jenna Sutherland's request when she asks him to use his position as a temporary FBI consultant to keep Claudia safe — especially because it's clear this little firecracker needs protecting. Far away from all the action she so craves, Claudia is more determined than ever to prove herself in her first major investigation at whatever cost — and those costs are proving to be dangerously high.

Their battle of wills turns quickly into a powerful need for one other, that makes them both rethink everything they ever wanted.

Will Trey be able to keep her alive long enough to give them an opportunity at something real together — a future that can survive the danger in their present, as well as the darkness of his past?

A STEEL TOWN SNEAK PEEK

Claudia's boots crunched over a smattering of dried leaves and gravel. The sound was almost thunderous against the silent backdrop of the abandoned steel mill site to which her very first tip had led her, forcing her to pause briefly, as the echoing noise dissipated. The delay was also helpful in allowing her racing heart to slow, if only a small amount.

Shadows overtook the many nooks and crevices of this metallic wasteland, as the ribbons of violet and dusky orange, which had been streaking above the length of the Ohio River, were rapidly surrendering to the much more inky and dark shades of twilight. With a shaky breath, she took out her phone to look at the satellite map images she'd collected before leaving her apartment. Claudia relied on the glow from her phone and made a quick left turn between two small buildings. They appeared to have once been designated for storage, but after years of neglect, the decrepit metal structures had become merely broken-down artifacts of a way of life long since departed from her new home of Pittsburgh. It had been decades since generations of workers reported there every day to craft the metal that formed the backbone of this city's development. Now its only visitors appeared to be graffiti artists, and perhaps the occasional drunk hoping to find a peaceful spot for his escape.

The entire scene was lonesome and anachronistic in a way that made her even more uncomfortable with the task she'd put upon herself. It also seemed like a damn fine place to get tetanus, so Claudia was treading carefully.

She put her phone away and zipped up her light leather jacket with slightly quivering fingers. The nighttime autumn air was crisp, seeping through her thin top, chilling her blood. It seemed to be so much colder down there by the river, the rusted out hulls of dozens of aluminum buildings creating a whistling wind tunnel that buffeted her small body with merciless cutting gusts.

This collapsing metal ghost town seemed a world away from the sparkling high rises of downtown Pittsburgh, and the tree lined brick streets of its historic neighborhoods. The beauty and quaintness of it all didn't make her frustration at her life being derailed by her brother any less suffocating. Yet, this evening jaunt was certainly making her appreciate the city's prettier face.

Calm down, she chastised herself. *I'm the one that wanted to be tough and act like a real agent. That means I need to suck it up, find the box the tipster told me about, and then I'm out of here.*

Her private pep talk seemed to work, steeling her nerves to keep walking with more confidence. With another sure-footed step, she turned sharply to maneuver between two more buildings.

Her feet, and her pulse, stopped short when a shadow flashed across the corner of her vision. At first, she could almost convince herself it was just her imagination, but she whipped her head around and saw a form ducking behind a corner. She caught enough of the view to see it was a man, tall and broad-shouldered beneath his hooded sweatshirt.

Claudia made sure her *Glock* was quickly accessible but she wanted to do all she could to avoid using it. This unwelcome visitor could be a danger, or the person behind her tip, or both. Seeing as she wasn't even supposed to be there, discharging her FBI-issued weapon was not a good idea. She took advantage of her petite frame and maneuvered forward delicately, venturing toward a more open area of the mill.

When the light was bright enough, she caught his shadow move more closely behind her.

Perfect.

With one quick motion, Claudia spun around with a roundhouse kick to his stomach. The muscles of his abs were firm beneath her blow, but she'd thrown him off balance, and had elicited quite a few expletives from him under his breath. Taking advantage of his distraction, Claudia threw herself on the ground. Supporting herself with her hands, she spun a low kick, taking him off his feet and landing him on his ass.

Worried he'd get back up, Claudia straddled him quickly and pinned his arms to the ground. It stunned her that he didn't fight her at all. *Perhaps he is still winded from my stomach kick?* she wondered.

Securing both his hands in one of hers as best she could, Claudia pushed his hood back from his face. Her breath skipped in her throat. The shadowy figure she'd just taken down was freaking gorgeous.

Dark hair framed his tanned face. He looked vaguely familiar, but she couldn't quite place him. Especially when she was distracted by the way his teasing curve of a smile and his sparkling gray eyes made it clear he was laughing at her. Still not uttering a word, he grinned fully at her and began to move his large torso to sit up and face her.

Aw, hell no, she thought. Moving her hands to his chest, she pushed him hard back to the ground.

"Hey, easy there, little tiger," he grunted out. "I let you have your fun, but this ground is starting to get uncomfortable. Even for a tough guy like me."

The smoothness of his voice, even through his clear annoyance, was almost hypnotic. His face held a few piercings and she could spy some tattoos peeking out from underneath his hoody, but he didn't look hard or dangerous — so much as intensely sexy. Finding a man this attractive was new to Claudia, and it was really pissing her off. Her eyes were too interested in his strong jaw and chiseled cheekbones, when they should be trying to determine if he was a threat. His face had a couple days of stubble, and she cursed herself for wondering what it would feel like on her fingers. *Would it be prickly, or smooth?*

"Are you done?" he asked.

"Excuse me?"

"Done staring at me?" he teased with a smile that revealed perfectly straight teeth resting behind his distracting lips.

"I-I'm not staring at you. I need to ascertain what kind of danger you are."

"Fine. Play it that way. You don't need to worry about me. I'm on your side."

"What? My side? Did Agent Jacobs figure out I was still going to follow up on this tip? Did he send you?"

"Agent Jacobs? Hell no. That dumb-ass wouldn't recognize a tip in a urinal."

"You're disgusting," Claudia snipped out, but his crass joke made a smile twitch at her lips.

"Besides, I'm not a Fed. Well, not really."

"Then who are you? Tell me who you are right now, or so help me…"

"So help you what? You'll swat at me with those little mitts of yours, again?"

Claudia lifted a fist and went at him hard. She wanted nothing more than to show him how those tiny paws of hers could do some serious damage, but he grabbed it in one of his large hands before she connected. She shook her hand out of his, fury pumping through her.

"You son of a bitch. Tell me who you are."

"Calm down. I'm Trey," he answered, awkwardly moving his other hand from his supine position to shake hers. "Nice to meet you, Agent McCoy...I think," he added. "I'm one of Jenna's friends." Claudia leaned back, sitting fully on his midsection as she processed this information.

"Wait. Trey? Trey *Adler*? Are you the one that's in love with my brother's live-in *girlfriend*, Jenna?"

"The Adler part is right. But I'm not in love with Jenna. What gave you that idea?"

"That's what Wyatt says."

"What your brother is wrong about is a lot."

"That may be true, but you still haven't told me what you're doing here."

"Um, first, do you mind moving...I know you're just a little thing..."

"I'm not little!"

"If you'd let me finish, I was going to say, no, you aren't that small. But if you don't climb off me we're going to have a situation on our hands. Or in my lap, to put it more accurately."

"You're a pig."

"You're the one that won't climb off me."

Claudia huffed at him, pushing off his chest hard enough to hear him release a satisfying, "oof" sound. Trey lifted a hand to her to help him up, his crooked grin never leaving his face.

She stared down at him for a minute, almost paralyzed.

"What? Aren't you strong enough?" he teased.

With an irritated sigh, she finally grabbed his hand with hers and helped him up from the ground. His hand fully enveloped her much smaller one. It was rough and cool to her touch. As soon as he was standing, Claudia dropped it like she'd been bitten. Now that he was standing fully in front of her, she had to crane her head back fully to meet his eyes.

"Impressive," he said softly. "You really are a pint-sized thing, aren't you? It was quite a pleasure letting you take me down."

"*Letting me?* Screw you." He just laughed gently in return. Claudia tried to bring reason back to her mind. "Why did Jenna ask you to follow me? What did she tell you?"

Shame coated Claudia's throat at the memory of letting herself get so sick in front of her brother's girlfriend — a stunning and confident physician, that knew a diabetic who couldn't handle her shit when she saw one.

Trey looked down at her, his eyes turning warm and reassuring. Claudia decided she preferred his teasing manner to this much more unsettling caring demeanor.

"Jenna didn't tell me anything. She didn't have to. She just asked and I said yes. I'm around the Pittsburgh FBI office a lot with the ongoing investigation into Jack Taylor's murder, so she figured I could keep an eye on you."

"I know that case. I've been trying to get on it. But they keep sticking me on the FBI equivalent of saving a cat stuck up in a tree. That's what…"

"This supposed lead is about? I know. I also know you were told not to follow up on it."

"Yeah. I get told 'no' quite a bit."

"I'm not a fan of being told what to do either, Claudia." It was the first time he'd said her name and it was like he'd poured warm honey down her body. "But that doesn't mean you shouldn't be careful. You were planning to follow up on a shady tip like that all alone?"

"I tried to get support, but they think it's a dumb idea."

"Instead you decided to come out here by yourself — a

place that looks like Murder City, population of you? Forget the danger factor for a second, do you know how much trouble that'll get you into with your boss?"

"So? From what I hear about you, all you do is get in trouble."

He stepped so closely to Claudia that he towered completely over her. The heat of his body came over her in waves, almost overwhelming her. Trey stared down at her until she met his eyes fully.

"*You* aren't *me*," he whispered.

"Thank goodness for that," she huffed out, turning to walk away briskly. Claudia raised her chin, desperately trying to remember her original path before this tattooed pain in the ass interfered with her evening, but it seemed like her brain just wouldn't work. A sudden tug at her right arm spun her around, forcing her to look up again, straight into his chiseled features.

"All right, that's it. Your whole feisty thing is cute, and all. But I promised Jenna I'd keep you alive, so I'll tell you right now — this shit's going to get old really quick."

"I'm so sorry to inconvenience you. Here's a solution. How about you leave me alone? Win-win, for both of us."

"Oh no, you don't, little one. Trust me, babysitting a spoiled McCoy sibling is not appealing to me in the slightest, but Jenna is a good friend and I can't say no to her."

"That does a lot for your whole 'I'm not in love with Jenna' thing."

Trey pressed a hand at the small of her back, stilling her.

"Are you scared I'm in love with Jenna, or that I'm not, and that my heart is available?"

"Oh please. I know your game. You just want to torment me. Thing is, if I don't get going, it'll get too dark to find anything, and this whole night will have been a waste."

"Not a total waste," he answered with a smile, "you got to meet me."

"Ugh, no wonder my brother hates you."

"Trust me, my feelings toward your brother are mutual. That doesn't change why I'm here, or what I promised I would do. If you won't give up, then you're just going to have to get used to me going everywhere you do."

Claudia turned away from him, but her stomach turned when she realized night had almost completely fallen. The mill yard had seemed manageable before, but now all she saw was a vast archipelago of treacherous alleys and easy hiding places. She'd come too far to turn back now, but doubt had crept into her bones, as insidiously as the rust that had slowly overtaken the building in front of her. "What's that they say in the movies?" Claudia muttered to herself. "Oh right. I've got a bad feeling about this."

"Me too. Do you want to leave now?"

"I'm not giving up. I never give up."

"Me neither," he answered.

A loud bang in the distance made her jump. She swallowed hard before choking out, "Fine. If you really want to come, I guess I can't stop you."

"How kind of you, because unfortunately for both of us, you're stuck with me. And I'm not going to let anything happen to you, little one."

ABOUT CHLOE T. BARLOW

Chloe is a contemporary romance novelist living in Pittsburgh, Pennsylvania with her husband and their sweet dog. She is a native Washingtonian that graduated *Duke University* with a degree in English and Chinese language. She met her husband at *Duke* and he brought her to Pittsburgh over a decade ago, which she has loved ever since and made her adopted hometown. She also attended the *University of Pittsburgh Law School* where she continued to be a book-loving nerd.

Chloe has always loved writing and cherishes the opportunity to craft her fictional novels and share them with the world. When Chloe isn't writing, she spends her time exploring Pittsburgh with her husband and friends. She also enjoys yoga, jogging, and all Pittsburgh sports, as well as her *Duke Blue Devils*.

She also thoroughly enjoys every opportunity to communicate with her readers. Since the release of her first two novels, *Three Rivers* and *City of Champions*, she has enjoyed the honor of meeting and talking with numerous fans, and looks forward to getting to know many more.

CONNECTING WITH CHLOE

If you enjoyed *Shanghai Wind*, or the other installments in the *Gateway to Love* series, please consider leaving reviews so that other readers can find them. Also, be sure to sign up for the Chloe T. Barlow newsletter. It is the best way to catch any deals, giveaways, new releases, or other exciting news about Chloe's creations. You are also welcome to join Chloe's street team, Chloe's Crew, on Facebook.

Newsletter and Blog:
http://chloetbarlow.com/newsletter/

Chloe enjoys nothing more than interacting with her readers, so please keep in touch!
Facebook:
https://www.facebook.com/ChloeTBarlow
Twitter:
https://twitter.com/chloetbarlow
Goodreads:
https://www.goodreads.com/author/show/7376511.Chloe_T_B arlow
Email:
chloe@chloetbarlow.com
Google+:
https://plus.google.com/u/0/116405903319564147007/posts
Chloe's Crew (Chloe Barlow Street Team):
https://www.facebook.com/groups/chloebarlowcrew/
Pinterest:
http://www.pinterest.com/chloetbarlow/
Amazon Author Page:
http://www.amazon.com/Chloe-T.-Barlow/e/B00IXAHC64/ref=ntt_athr_dp_pel_1

28915779R00066

Made in the USA
Middletown, DE
05 February 2016